WIZEN
WOODS

VELVET DAVIS

*To the Hoh Rainforest, for inspiring
me to write this book.*

WHEN THE OLD seer spoke, his words became one with the stylus in Raela's hand. The stylus moved effortlessly, as if his speech melted onto the page in front of the young girl.

Her fingers glided with ease, recording with a lightness she had not known her fingers could possess. They moved with a power she was somehow separate from. As it happened, it felt all too natural. It wasn't until later that she marveled at the swiftness of her hand, the moments when it progressed even faster than her comprehension of his spoken words.

Mist hung like a shroud, protecting them from distraction. The blurred trees and scenery suggested there was nothing beyond what they were doing. Whether this was an intentional ploy by nature itself to keep them focused was a question left unanswered. As always, nature left her mysteries for those who wished to ponder them. And they did not.

There came a time during his speech when the seer became troubled. Deep creases stretched across his forehead, and words fell from his mouth in broken pieces. Before long, they oozed from his lips like pus. Raela started when she realized the implication of his words. Even as a child, she understood the horror. As their meaning became ever more disturbing, she grew bewildered, but her hand was stubborn and continued. A chill from the air encircled them, and Raela shivered while her hand traveled steadily before her.

So while the prophecy bled from his lips, her hand caught it and projected it onto the page. No small feat for such a young girl, but it fit her character well. She had been born to record ideas, so her grandfather had told her. She came from a long line of scribes—recorders of her people's ways.

Yet the birthmark on her thumb proved that she was special.

When her grandfather's prophetic words ceased, and it came time to close the book, thereby preserving its thick pages, she did so with careful grace. A symbol now glowed on its cover—signifying its completion. And no one besides their fiercest warrior, not yet of age himself, would deny the power emanating from its light.

CHAPTER ONE

SECLUDED WITHIN MILES of primeval forest, a fire danced wildly in the night. It threw shadows all around the clearing, and though fires usually brought her peace, Raela instead felt a sinister vibe emanating from its flames.

She shivered.

One should not be cold standing near a fire.

She stepped closer until the heat lashed at her skin. Flames stretched high above her, like giant claws attempting to reach the stars peeking between branches or perhaps even rip them from the sky.

The gathering had yet to begin, and she was surprised by her nervousness, for this was a ceremony she took part in every year. Still, her stomach trembled uneasily, and she struggled to tame her thoughts.

Members of the tribe entered the clearing from the narrow dirt path that led from the village. They gathered around the fire, some settling onto the warped log benches that had been there for as long as she could remember.

Her grandfather stood with his gnarled cane where the path met the clearing, conversing with those who paused to greet him. His demeanor was tempered by the shades of gray rimming his features. Beneath the animal skins wrapped around him, his stance resembled a rickety old tree. But she knew his mind was as sharp as it was the day she'd written the prophecy down for him.

The prophecy lay on the jagged stone outcropping—a leather-bound book with thick pages. On its cover, the strange symbol glowed just as intensely as the fire. It always gave her pause, this symbol, for it was not one she had put there. It had appeared once the words were recorded, as if to signify its own importance or to clinch an agreement of some kind. There was no other explanation for its existence.

Raela did not acknowledge the others, for her grandfather stole their attention as the tribal seer. When he spoke, others listened, even when he was only engaging in pleasantries.

She only half-listened, for her mind was very far away, huddled within a deep pondering from which she could not break free. Though perhaps her awareness was not as far away as she had thought.

Raela.

The whisper came from the darkness outside the glow of the fire.

She stiffened. Though she knew who called for her, it would not do well to give the others something to gossip about. The seer's granddaughter, the one who had written down the prophecy, must not allow herself to be distracted on the day she must present the book to him.

Careful not to draw the others' notice, she cautiously turned her head.

Outside the clearing, a figure masked by shadows took advantage of a small pocket of light and motioned for her to follow. She stood discreetly and crept away from her place in the bright circle. Slipping into the trees, she followed him into the night. He tiptoed lightly away, his feet pressing the ground in artful silence, maintaining a short distance ahead of her—drawing her further and further away from the others and their warm fire.

The crickets chirping and distant howls drowned out the sound of wood crackling. The chill increased. Perhaps she would have been wise to wrap herself in blankets before exiting her hut, but she did not have the foresight of her grandfather.

Finally, when they were safely out of view from the rest of the tribe, and the trees and brush softened the sounds they continued to make, he turned abruptly and waited for her to close the gap between them. His features were barely visible, but his eyes gazed at her with a sharp intensity that rivaled the fire behind them.

Their lips met in the cool twilight. He placed his arms around her. They kissed a slow, lingering kiss that made her forget about her earlier wish of having a blanket to warm her. He broke away from her after several seconds of elation passed, mere inches, to gaze meaningfully into her eyes. Yet she was the first to speak.

"Rebial," she said breathlessly. "Your kiss is fickle. It brings both pleasure and trouble."

"Only if they saw you leave," he replied, "will it bring trouble."

"Someone always sees," she said. "And that's not entirely what I mean by trouble."

"What were you doing back there?" he asked, playfully tugging at her wrists to draw her closer.

Wondering when he would tire of this yearly game, she laughed.

"You know what I was doing," she replied. "I was getting ready to present the prophecy to my grandfather. The ceremony is about to begin."

Her response seemed rehearsed, even to her.

"Why is it," Rebial teased, "that neither you nor the tribe ever tire of this ceremony?"

"Why would we tire of celebrating something that will help our people survive?"

"I know all about survival," Rebial said. "Don't forget my own ceremony will be held soon. I will become a warrior, and you will look to me for survival."

With his shoulders so broad before her, she did not doubt this. She smiled at his protectiveness, certain he would make a fine warrior. Yet she was also disappointed that he undermined her involvement in something so important to the tribe.

"That may be," she said, "but would it hurt you to support me in this?"

Only as a young woman had she begun to defend herself.

"The elusive prophecy," he replied, dodging her point. "Always hanging over us. Always reminding us that our descendants will be forced to crawl like insects beneath the ground, instead of fighting back like the warriors that we are."

"Not everyone was born to fight."

"Yet we are quite adept at it, aren't we? We've successfully defended our homeland all this time."

"So then why not be happy that the time the prophecy warns us of is still far in the future?" she said with a smile.

This truth always lightened the argument.

"That is the only thing I like about the prophecy," he said, gently kissing her. "That its time is in the future."

"A burden for our children to bear," she replied, turning her head to avoid another kiss.

They had been lingering for too long. Her duty awaited her.

"Must you go back already?" he asked mischievously, as if to tempt her one last time with his charming smile.

"The time has come," she said, backing away slowly, "for me to hand the prophecy to my grandfather."

She turned away, then paused. "Will you watch?" she asked over her shoulder.

"No," he replied, "I'll be in the woods."

She sighed, knowing he probably would watch, shaded by trees. What else did he have to do?

Sliding back into the clearing, she drew the eyes of those who sat nearby. They gave her knowing looks and whispered to each other. Her relationship with Rebial had never been a secret, nor had he kept his opinions of the prophecy to himself. This controversy followed her at all times.

But she had her role despite all this. No one else's opinion could change who she was.

She joined her grandfather at the forefront of the gathering. Only when she stood beside him did he gesture for the chanting to begin, along with the subtle yet underlying beating of the drums. The tribal members designated for these tasks obeyed, causing the mood to change from casual to reverent.

The others ceased their conversation as the hypnotic sound filled the clearing. They looked at Raela and her grandfather attentively.

She lifted the book from the table, felt its energy emanate into her fingertips.

Then, with a small grin, she handed her grandfather the book.

He held the book over his head, causing the symbol on its cover to gleam with the same brightness as the stars above them.

"We have gathered once again to celebrate what nature has given us—the gift of prophecy."

Sounds of gratitude spilled from the lips of those in attendance as they listened.

"It will save us," the seer continued, "from the horrors that will destroy our world."

Her task fulfilled, Raela walked quietly to a vacant log near the fire and sat. No one paid attention to her now as her grandfather commanded their attention with gripping words that she had memorized, for he said nearly the same thing every year.

"I had a vision last night," her grandfather said dramatically, still holding the book up before the tribe. "It clarifies when the prophecy's time will come."

Her breath stilled. These were words she had not heard before…

A giant hush swept through the tribe as well, for this news was something they had all been waiting for. Years had passed since the prophecy had come into existence, and its time was always set in the future. Finally, they would know which one of their children or grandchildren would have to live life underground and away from the majestic forest that had been their home longer than the stories of their past stretched behind them.

Raela's thoughts raced anxiously. Would it be one hundred years or maybe two? Would it be her own children forced to regress or perhaps her grandchildren? Would she be forced to make the journey as an old woman? Would Rebial have time to rethink his opinion and walk proudly beside her, leaving all his second thoughts behind in the forest which was destined to be destroyed?

Her grandfather's pause was long, giving everyone time to gather their thoughts and composure. But something so far in the future should, by design, already have coping time built in, so why was he stalling like this?

"All this time," he continued, "we believed that the prophecy warned of a time far into the future, that its threats were a long time in coming. But last night, my vision told me something quite different. The people that I saw entering the cave and traveling through the tunnels…those people were us."

Raela felt a cold pressure bear down on her as her mind raced with panic.

"The time, I am sad to say, is upon us. The time has come to obey its wishes and follow the path it has outlined. Soon the signs will be apparent to us all."

Raela's heart broke into a thousand pieces, its shards slicing into her at different spots inside her body. She clenched her hands and held them tightly against her stomach to staunch the pain.

The reaction amongst the other tribal members was varied—some joined the chanting, some muttered empty words of anguish, while others cried and held the hands of nearby loved ones—but all this remained in the background of Raela's awareness.

The only person she truly saw was Rebial standing amid the trees ringing the clearing, watching her. His figure, framed in vegetation, was distorted by the flames. The anger writhing on his face matched the raging fire between them.

So he had been watching. He could not stay away for long; he never did. And now he would be forced to accept the prophecy he disbelieved and hated. He would be alive to witness the defeat of his forest.

"We must not feel sorry for ourselves," her grandfather continued, "for this should be a happy time. Although we will be forced to live out much of our existence in ways we'd never have chosen, we have still been given life. We will survive this turmoil."

Raela sat dumbly, unable to fully process the news that continued to tear her thoughts into fragments and eat away at her heart.

She looked up again, but Rebial no longer stood beyond the wicked glow. Or perhaps his hate had grown so strong that he had merged with the flame.

And she knew then that the hollow pit that had formed inside her stomach would never be filled. Because of this news, her life would never be the same.

The fire snapped and crackled as if to chuckle at her pain.

CHAPTER TWO

RAELA SAT STILL beside the fire, like the stone she would become beneath the ground. The news settled like dust overtop her. The fire continued to taunt, spitting embers onto the grass near her feet. The threat seemed meager. It did not provoke her to move away.

Perhaps the sting would jolt her from the shocking nightmare she now found herself in.

Members of the tribe milled about in a hyper frenzy. Bits and pieces of conversation met her ears, most indistinguishable from one to the other, until the casual words of a tribal elder cut through her subconscious like a knife.

"We will cancel the rite of passage ceremony," he said decisively to his companion. "There's no need for warriors beneath the ground."

Raela didn't know if anyone saw her, nor was it a conscious decision to remove herself from the gathering, but she soon found herself chasing shadows in the woods, searching for Rebial.

Somehow she found him—perhaps her intuition moved in alignment with her heart—standing within a cluster of trees that made his powerful figure appear slight. Face glowing in the moonlight, he scowled when he saw her.

"Rebial," she said softly. "I have bad news."

"Do you think I'm deaf?" he asked harshly. "I heard."

No," she replied quickly, "I saw you—"

"The prophecy's time has come!" Rebial cut her off. "How does he know?"

"He is the seer," she hissed. "The future comes to him in dreams and visions."

"Yet he tells you that you share the same gift. What do you see?"

It was a valid question. Raela tentatively approached the place inside her mind that she supposed would house such visions. But she only found the same hazy cloud that continued to let her down.

"I see nothing," she admitted. "I do not have these visions. I thought the prophecy would be a burden to bear for our descendants."

Rebial's eyes lit up, oblivious to her feelings of awkwardness or perhaps not caring that her sight remained obscured.

"Perhaps the time has come to pass the torch to you then. His mind is decaying and yours is fresh and bright."

"You do not understand," she replied. "I do not think I have the sight."

"Then I am correct. Your grandfather sees things that do not exist. His visions will never come into fruition." Rebial smirked at her, pleased with his revelation.

Raela frowned. How dare he use her personal failings as a weapon against her. "You must accept it. You have to."

Rebial narrowed his eyes. "Accept it like the rest of the tribe? That survival coincides with hiding? That the answer to our problems is to live like cowards? That we should let evil overtake our homeland?"

Raela turned away. "It merely says that we are to regress," she said, voice faltering. "It does not measure our days more so than that."

"To me, that means concede defeat," he replied.

But they had fought this fight many times before. Her grandfather had advised her that Rebial could not be swayed. Yet she would continue to try, for now, she had no choice. And she was determined to tell him the news, which would surely succeed at breaking down his stubbornness eventually.

"You focus on one thing only," she said. "Why not focus on the positive? We must stay hidden so that nature can shield us. She wants us to stay safe."

"That's not a positive thing. It's an outrage. Your grandfather's interpretation is insulting. Please tell me you have finally recognized how foolish it is. Nature does not reward those who do nothing."

"Actually, I remain a strong believer. How else will our people survive the treachery that will befall our homeland? And the planet?"

"Treachery," he spat the word back out at her. "It would be more treacherous if our people actually stooped to believe such nonsense."

"Seer is trustworthy. And he is my grandfather," she reminded him. "Everything else he has foreseen has come true. Why would he be wrong now?" She placed her hands on her hips to emphasize her stern expression.

"I can accept an evil is upon us. Or else the book would not exist. I do not accept that our only choice is retreat."

He looked back at her defiantly. His dominance overpowered her. So was the way with her lover. His fierce pride could at once emanate from his body yet stay retained within him. His character was so strong that it stole the strength of others. Her own strength slipped weakly away as he stood largely before her.

But just because his passion ran so strong didn't mean that she was incorrect.

"Have you no respect for our elder? How can you minimize all he has achieved?" she finally asked.

"I had respect for him," Rebial replied, "but he is misreading the signs. His mind is not what it used to be. He is getting too old to be advising our people."

"I do not think so," she replied, shaking her head. "My grandfather is still shrewd and clever. He deserves even more respect now that he is saving us from what's to come."

"Saving us? That frail old man? Are you telling me that you would place the fate of our people, and even your own, in the hands of a man who is so weak he can barely lift a pipe to his lips? When you could be under the protection of me, the strongest and most skilled fighter of our entire tribe?"

"Do not liken brains with brawn," she countered.

"Do not underestimate me," he was quick to retort. "My brain is a fair match of any other."

"Yes, but you are not as wise as my grandfather."

Her words met a stiff silence, so she continued, "And wisdom is what will save us inside the cave."

His glare fully actualized, she knew its hate was not intended for her.

"I thought the prophecy would save us," he said.

"It will," she said, pressing her lips firmly together, "which is why I think the elders decided to…"

The right words failed to reach her mouth, and she swallowed to fill the silence.

"Decided to what?"

"Cancel the warrior ceremony," she said.

Shaking his head in disgust, he said, "You go too far."

"I'm telling you the truth. I heard them whispering before I came to find you. Otherwise, I would have let you sulk."

"So my fate has been decided for me then," he said bitterly, "because of a book dreamed up by a seer."

"Just because you don't like what it says doesn't mean that it's not true," she replied.

"Am I the only one who doesn't like all that it says? What about the passage that—"

"Shhh!" Raela pressed a finger to her lips in warning. "We do not discuss these things."

The topic they would not discuss hung between them, silencing them, until after several moments, it faded back into the recesses of their minds where it belonged.

"I can't believe you would accept it." He locked eyes with her. "Just like I can't believe you are as weak-minded as the rest."

He backed away from her then, melting into the darkness between trees. Within seconds he was no longer visible, and she felt vastly alone. The whirring sounds of insects filled her ears, vibrating in her eardrums, while fresh tears blurred the murk around her.

Now that Rebial was gone, had left her to fend for herself in the unpredictable night, an uneasiness overcame her. Though she wished to remain by herself, it would be best to go back to the others before the feline hunters sniffed her out and took advantage of her solitude.

She turned to rejoin the gathering, walking only a few feet toward the glow of the distant fire before hearing a shuffle of a sound nearby. Had he returned to mend the rift between them?

"Don't trouble yourself over that one," an unsavory voice said. "He cannot be changed."

Quite fittingly, its owner remained in the shadows.

"Mind your business, Vandor," Raela snapped before hurrying angrily away, her mood now matching the vivid flame of her destination.

A rogue like him would bring her no comfort. She knew what he liked to do to wounded things.

CHAPTER THREE

REBIAL MOVED SWIFTLY through the darkness with the night vision of a hunter. The big cats did not scare him. Nor did the other creatures that lurked within the shadows all around. If he were prone to fear, he would not deserve to become a warrior—the title he was so stubborn to attain no matter the cost.

Raela had to be messing with him. The elders would not deny him of this right.

With his sight restricted to the narrow path outlined in silhouettes of vegetation, he relied on his senses to gauge his whereabouts. He knew the forest so well he could walk it in his sleep. For that matter, he actually did move through it in his dreams.

The forest was inside him the same way as he was inside of it. It sustained the health of both his body and his mind. This bond he shared with his surroundings was stronger than any he had shared with any other human, even Raela.

His ancestors whispered to him as he passed their haunts. Even their ghoulish nagging did not spook him. He was certain they were encouraging him. He couldn't fathom they would be proponents of his tribe leaving the forest, allowing their memories to rot away with the rest of the world. Not when it could be stopped. Not when he possessed the power to stop it. His pride shared the girth of the greatest tree, his confidence matched its heights.

How his tribe could be content to leave their homeland was a strange mystery to him—savage in its own way. Unthinkable. Treasonous to their very existence. Their homeland was more than just a place, more than just a setting in the background. He stooped to pick up a stone nestled in dirt that glinted in the moonlight.

Staring at its ruddy imperfections, he tried to envision living a good portion of his existence within its solid walls. The inside of a stone never saw the sun, much like the inner workings of a cave. In fact, caves were much the macrocosm of a stone. And he could not imagine himself being trapped inside one for an unfathomable length of time, so long that time itself would grow bored of those trapped within its constraints.

Raela had mentioned the prophecy claimed that if the book was brought beneath the ground, kept within the inner circle of the tribe by its keeper, that a generation would not pass. And his people's patience would be rewarded when they were allowed to emerge again—having endured a wait that would be as grueling as watching a river fill drop by drop.

But patience was not Rebial's strength. It seemed a painful thing to do, be locked inside a stone beneath the ground while waves of destruction happened above. He did not think that he could wait so peacefully, out of sight of the sky and the towering trees, to accommodate the misconceptions of an old man—one who could so easily accept the frayed hope of safety as opposed to choosing life within the heat of battle.

He could not appreciate trading a life filled with purpose and excitement for one characterized by a long, boring yet safe existence.

The forest was more than just their home; it was special. It revealed its nature both by what it alluded to and what it exposed in plain sight.

He was not surprised that it had relayed this future to the tribe. The wood was prone to secrets as evidenced by all the tunneling burrows that led to places no one could go. Each tree rose uniquely like a separate thought. There were small nooks within their trunks where things could hide. Even the caves beneath the spidery root legs could house things in tucked away spots that were impossible to see.

He could sense the riddle in its roots that meandered across the forest floor. A falling vine trailed like a lingering thought.

The trees spoke to each other through the roots and mycelium that spread throughout the forest floor. A flower could accept a secret from a bee. The bee would then scatter the response as it flew to far corners.

Creatures hid in plain sight so effectively, with skin that matched their surroundings, suggesting there was much more to a forest than the eye could see if one would only take the time to look.

Even plants hoarded secrets if one cared enough to find them. The powers hidden within their green and leafy forms could cure, comfort, and even bring one bliss.

Mushrooms sprouted quickly when necessary to do so, but these beings were more mysterious and secretive than most. New types were always emerging in sporadic places with no known rhyme or reason to their whims, and for the most part, their specific purposes remained unknown.

Trees made pictures in their shapes, of giant beasts or rickety figures emerging from splintered bark. They told stories with these shapes, reminding him of a time long past when trickster gods and terrible creatures roamed—before the advent of humans forced them into subtle memories as myths and legends.

So, yes, he did agree the forest had revealed a secret to his tribe, which had been picked up on by their seer. Or perhaps it was the driving force of all things, the keeper of the planet—an entity his father had often mentioned to him—who revealed these secrets through the forest to keep its people safe. Longevity was their reward for being loyal and having reverence for the wood, their reward for being the ones the planet chose to keep safe by revealing that their home was about to be invaded.

But leaving their homeland behind to suffer whatever damages the invaders brought to it seemed more than negligent. It was like betraying the one who had taken care of you all this time.

For Rebial, it had. The forest had been there like a faithful friend when his father had passed away. It had consoled him when his mother had followed soon after.

These memories forced his knees to buckle. They ground into the cool soil, a sensation he found strangely comforting. For it was not the warmth in a forest that brought calmness to his mind, but instead these cool, mothering touches of serenity.

He looked up at the branches glittering above him, noticed a branch bending up and down with the breeze as if to gesture him upward.

He stood and continued walking. Each step bathed in moonlight, his mind relaxed further, and he decided it was time to seek his bed inside his hut.

Someone stepped into his path as he made his way back to the village. Though the darkness marred his sight, Rebial could sense the nature of the man who stood before him, obstructing his path. His lip curled in distaste. This invader of his privacy pried with an unashamed curiosity that was unwelcome in most cases, for Vandor was a man who poked and prodded death.

They had crossed paths many times before in ways that were not amicable. Rebial was quick to eat his kill while Vandor merely studied a corpse, allowing it to rot so the tribe could not use its body for food or anything beneficial. He'd begun using animal remains in ways that went beyond the realm of need and instead hinged on rabid curiosity. It was a twisted practice, heavily frowned upon by others, and Vandor had fallen out of favor since. Some even considered him sick in the head.

Wrapped in animal skins like most members of the tribe, though Rebial chose not to think about the circumstances of these deaths, Vandor seemed to be wearing, quite literally, who he was on his sleeve.

Rebial had threatened Vandor before when he'd caught him examining the insides of an animal whose carcass did not appear to have been nibbled upon by any predators, nor was it an animal that the tribal members typically ate, for its meat was course and unsavory.

Vandor had denied doing the killing, but Rebial suspected he was too liberal with the truth, for he had not provided a satisfying alternative to the accusation. And since there were certain things Rebial found unforgivable, the relationship between the men was tenuous at best.

After a thorough interrogation by the tribal elders, Vandor had confessed to slaughtering the animal to study it—a betrayal of the virtues of the tribe. One did not kill to examine, for this was a waste of an animal's remains and an insult to its spirit. And it did not bode well for the spirit of the one who'd done the killing.

As it was in most cases, Vandor's curiosities could be satisfied if he took the time to look deeper within himself. Though he claimed this was superstition, an inadequate solution based on myth alone.

The elders had reprimanded Vandor, and he'd supposedly ceased his abnormal inquiries. But the others still viewed him warily when he was in their midst and interacted with caution. And he and his clan—the small percentage with the same interests, though it was assumed this was encouraged by their leader—held a grudge against Rebial for exposing Vandor's hobbies. So not only was he disdainful, but he was also surprised that Vandor would appear before him.

Begrudgingly, he acknowledged Vandor with a pathetic mutter as he walked past.

Vandor moved quickly to fall into step beside him.

"I do not feel that you are being treated fairly," Vandor said, as if kindness were a normal thing between them.

"What do you mean?" Rebial asked impatiently.

"The tribal elders…did you not hear?" Vandor feigned surprise.

Rebial said grimly, "And so she was correct."

How could they do this to him? It was akin to breaking his spirit not to let him fulfill his destiny.

"The elders do not realize their mistake," Vandor said.

The conversation was already growing tedious. Vandor's pestering felt like a small child tugging at his sleeve.

"Your fake sympathy will not persuade me to side with your despicable ways."

"Can a man never escape an action he regrets?"

"Do you regret it?" Rebial could not help but ask the question with a sharp tongue.

Vandor paused before admitting, "I do regret that I was misjudged."

"That's what I thought." Rebial quickened his pace, yet Vandor refused to be left behind.

"My exploration was altruistic," he said, keeping up with short, quick steps. "How do the insides of an animal work? I would suspect they're much like ours. And if that's the case, what wonders we could do with that knowledge."

Disgust washed over Rebial as he remembered the scent of the carcass involved in Vandor's study. Or whatever you call spending hours staring at death rather than burying it or preparing it for food. An act that refrains from using the animal parts for a purpose and instead just watches the rot occur.

"It's true you may get knowledge from studying death," Rebial replied, "but when you have a forest full of plants that aid in treating ailments, there is no reason to wonder about such things."

"Is there not? Or do you fail to understand me? Like the elders fail to understand you?"

Now Rebial felt the verbal attack—the knife sliding through his skin. He knew there had to be a motive in Vandor's methods. He was sure he was about to find out what it was.

"Do not compare yourself to me," he replied.

"I wouldn't dare compare myself to a man who has suffered the way you have, losing your father and then your mother at such a young age."

Rebial stiffened as the knife twisted now, causing damage. Yet as anger rose within him, he refused to let Vandor's handiwork be seen and instead continued walking briskly.

"There was no plant inside the forest that could fix him," Vandor continued. "And yet, perhaps if we knew how our insides worked, something could have been done to save him."

Rebial remembered watching the healer try herb after herb, plant after plant, but to no avail. His father had worsened. And his gaping wound had turned black with infection. At one point, the healer admitted there was nothing left to try.

As they'd told Rebial the devastating news, his father had held firmly onto his hand, did not even flinch. He had fought his last battle, protected the tribe one last time, and had accepted his impending death.

"My father had made peace with dying," Rebial said matter-of-factly.

"So he had. But don't you think he would have liked to see his child grow?"

Rebial considered how his father would react were he alive to witness what was happening—the seer's cowardly interpretation of the prophecy. But he would not give Vandor the satisfaction of a real response. This man, so unlike his father, had worn out his welcome long ago.

"What do you want, Vandor?"

"I just want to let you know I understand how it feels to be misunderstood. And I wouldn't blame you for whatever you decide."

This implied Rebial had a choice, which he did. He just hadn't realized that the workings of his mind were on such display to the rest of the tribe.

Someone always sees, Raela had said…

"I have decided nothing—"

"You have not decided to stay behind and avenge your homeland? Don't lie to me. You are the son of a warrior. Don't tell me you aren't considering it."

Rebial cringed, realizing his mistake of letting his emotions show. Not tonight, but in obvious to subtle ways throughout his existence. Everyone knew how he viewed the prophecy, and now he was forced to face his opinion head-on. Would he react as predictably as Vandor suggested? Would he choose to stay behind?

If word got out that he was considering this, before he'd even discussed it with Raela, she would never forgive him. And she may not choose to stay beside him. It would be ideal to make the suggestion on their time, perhaps during a cuddle in the treetops together. If she did decide to stay with him, he would protect her at all costs. His forest and his wife, keeping them safe, would be his mission in life.

If she left the wood, well, there was nothing he could do to keep her safe—not if his spirit had a say in the matter.

"I have decided nothing," he said more firmly now. "I am just doing what I would be doing if life were normal."

"Of course you are," Vandor said, in a way that would deter snakes emerging from a burrow. "But if you do decide to stay behind, it may not be the worst choice. Just because someone fails to understand you doesn't mean that you are wrong."

Leaves rustled in the cool breeze that wafted past. Was the sudden chill a warning from the wood?

"I do not need your understanding," Rebial said. "But perhaps you should stay behind to study the death that the prophecy claims will spread across the planet."

He instantly regretted his words. Vandor was the last person he wanted to be spending any time with or dying alongside of. But ironically, self-preservation was Vandor's greatest motivation, despite his interest in the decomposition of animals.

"Don't think I haven't considered it," he said, his steps slowing. "Oh, I have. But no matter what you think, I respect death. I know how it must feel based on my examinations. And no matter what you think, the purpose of my studies is to evade it. I do not wish to fall within its clutches just yet."

Rebial used a branch to swing himself over a rift, finally creating the distance he was sure Vandor wasn't skilled enough to cross.

"Then it would be in your best interest to make your way back to the village," he said over his shoulder, "and be safe in the company of others."

Alone now, he wound deeper into the shimmering woods. Let Vandor interpret that however he wished.

CHAPTER FOUR

AFTER A NIGHT that tortured him with restless sleep, Rebial decided to confront the tribal elders inside the giant thatched hut in which they congregated every morning. Now standing within their sacred circle, surrounded by all seven of them, he did not bother hiding the resentment he was sure emanated from his face.

He could not even view them as men. They were obstacles, barriers, depriving him of the warrior status that was rightfully his. They held his destiny captive, made a mockery of his entire existence by belittling all he had trained for. He had already said as much to them, and though he sensed nervousness in their demeanors—for he knew he was imposing—there was also an unyielding assuredness in their decision. They would not bend. For this, he hated them.

"We regret we have to alter tradition, disregard your warrior lineage and deny you of your rite of passage, but we must obey the prophecy," an elder said in a stern manner.

"Our traditions should persist," Rebial countered.

"The prophecy has changed the way our tribe will function," the elder said, "both underground and in the future that comes after."

"The prophecy," Rebial spat out, "is only a gathering of words on paper, dreamed up by a seer who has outlived his worth."

"You mustn't fall prey to disrespect," the same elder responded harshly.

Rebial scowled at the elder, whose choice of wording seemed all too contrived. Comparing him to prey only added insult to injury. And a warrior, when injured, needed to fight back strongly before the injury weakened him further.

"I only disrespect those who deserve it," he said. "The prophecy is a weak old man's solution to our upcoming problems. My men and I are more than capable of thwarting any attacks on our homeland. Let the fearful run and hide. The strong can stay and fight."

His friends had to have felt it—the bitter burning from the elders repressing who they were destined to become.

"You no longer have any men," the elder said. "Unlike you, they have accepted their fate. Both the old and the young have come to terms with this development."

Fire ignited in his gut, for this was news to him. "I don't need the loyalty of my friends to determine my own fate. Nor do I need them at all, for that matter."

"Well then, in that case, it appears you also have no friends," the elder replied flippantly.

This insult steadied him, gave him confidence, for he was no stranger to isolation.

"I do not require companionship," he said. "Nor do I require your consent. I do, however, ask for it one last time. So that I can share the same title as my father and my grandfather."

The elders stared at him, and for a moment, he thought his fierce passion had infected them. He could see the fading light within their eyes, their wish that what they thought must come to pass would not have to be, so they could continue living their happy ways. It was a good life they shared with the forest and each other. But one by one, they shook their heads.

"You will always be the son of one of our greatest warriors," the head elder said slowly, "but a warrior, yourself, you will never be."

Anger tore at his composure, and he shook from the force of it. "Then I will claim the title myself. I will call myself a warrior."

"Only the elders can hand out such a title. And we are refusing your request."

"I'm not asking," Rebial replied. "I'm demanding your cooperation."

"And we are answering not evading," said a different elder in a reasonable tone. "You must accept our decision. There is nothing else you can do."

"It is time for you to accept the fate the prophecy has given you," the head elder said.

Rebial twisted his mouth into a grim smirk. "That sentiment may pacify you, but it doesn't console me. If I can't become a warrior, then you watch"—he glared darkly—"what I do become."

The elders were silent as he turned his back on them. His father had taught him that a warrior never relents in the heat of battle. And so he would not.

His mind made up, he left their sacred circle, walking briskly from the hut. They did not control him. There was nothing they could do to stop him if he stayed behind to avenge the wood. He could live the life of a warrior without their approval.

While this was true, was he really brave enough to do this alone?

He stalked past the surrounding huts, drawing the attention of many who paused from their chores to watch with expressions that managed to annoy him further. His resentment mingled with anger, but he refused to meet anyone's gaze.

He'd had enough of the gossip and judgments that came with the tribal way of life. Being part of a whole could at times be a burden when one preferred a life of solitude. Wouldn't the forest be enough to sustain him? Did he really need the other members of the tribe when they routinely brought him more grief than pleasure?

The village shrank behind him as he entered the cool embrace of the woods. Surrounded by lush and familiar vegetation, his anger softened. Branches dipped down within his line of sight, as if they were stroking him with each passing step.

How could the elders—mere men—deny him of his birthright? With his father's passing, he was next in line to lead the tribe against any threat, including invaders. He'd known this even as a child, for his father had ingrained this into his psyche. The intention had been to train his son even better than he, himself, could fight.

So much so that even in Rebial's dreams, there was no peace. He was forever stalking, prowling, and protecting. If he could not contain his fighting spirit even when asleep, how could he ignore it tucked away inside the planet for years on end?

"Remember," his father had told him one crisp morning as they practiced throwing spears. "Sometimes, the hardest part of being a warrior is knowing when to stop fighting."

"Why would a warrior stop fighting?" Rebial had asked.

"He would stop fighting when it benefits his people, when the fighting causes more harm than good. When the sacrifice outweighs the benefits of the battle."

As a young boy in this memory, Rebial had considered this as he gripped onto the spear. At the time, he did not quite understand the wisdom of the words, but somehow, he could sense their significance. He drew his arm back, weighed the spear overhead, then thrust it from his grip. It sailed forward and stuck squarely in the tree knot he had aimed at. He looked at his father for praise, a proud look on his face.

"Well done, son," he'd said with a nod. "However, exactness is a skill that comes easy when not in the throes of battle. Try again."

Confused, Rebial lifted another spear from the pile at his feet. Why try again under the same circumstances, he wondered, when clearly his father was less than impressed?

He took aim, but this time his father lifted a spear and touched its tip to Rebial's throat.

He started, eyes widening, but his father's voice penetrated his fears.

"Is it difficult to concentrate now?" he asked.

"Yes," Rebial had whispered.

"Now, imagine if an enemy was upon you and that fear was real. Concentration during those moments is most crucial."

Rebial aimed and his spear flew forward. It hit the bark a few inches to the right of his target. He sighed at himself in disgust, shoulders slumping in disappointment.

His father lowered the spear from Rebial's throat. "You missed the heart but still did damage."

"I am not satisfied with only inflicting damage," he protested.

His father shrugged. "Sometimes that's all it takes."

"When can I fight a real battle, Father?"

"You can fight a real battle when one arises," his father said simply.

"But we have enemies. Can't we start one?"

"No." His father's voice was stern. "That's another important trait of a good warrior. A warrior only fights when the need arises, not to satisfy a whim."

"There is honor," his father continued, "in being a warrior. Remember that."

Mulling this memory alongside his current situation, he paced dirt paths that wound around trees with ragged bark. His only destination was the goal of clarification. Each path was like him analyzing a thought. It led to another, as ruminations do, and he walked the maze that had erupted inside his mind.

In a maze, there are no answers, yet there is only one way out. He was certain he would find it, though it may not lead to where he truly wanted to go.

If he did find the answer, would it be a satisfying ending to this conundrum he found himself in?

Each thought was edged with giant trees, just like the path before him. The forest was embedded in him, its roots wrapped securely around his passion.

Only if his homeland is under attack does a warrior fight.

The pain of his father's death was still raw in his heart. It coursed through him at the mere remembrance. His father had not sought death, but it had come for him, and he had accepted its wrath with calm complacency. The greatest warrior of the tribe had viewed his own passing in the old way, fought to the death, allowed himself to be a sacrifice for the good of his people.

Though the act had been noble, and his father was still revered for it, Rebial recalled how the act had affected him. He and his mother were left to fend for themselves. And some other warrior had taken his father's place until Rebial was old enough to claim the status that was rightfully his. Had Rebial been nearer the age of a young man, the only setback would have been dealing with the pain of his loss.

But no, instead, his mother had borne the brunt of this sacrifice and died of a broken heart only a few years later. Her loss had been easier to bear, but only because he was already so numb inside. Fortunately, by then, he was close enough to the age of a young man that he could take care of himself and stay in his family's hut.

The greatest honor of a warrior is to die protecting your homeland.

Rebial would sacrifice himself all the same. He would stay and fight, regardless of what anyone said. He would fight until the death, ending his life just as nobly as his father had done.

He would not crawl through tunnels like an animal and wait for the threat to pass. He refused to live beneath the soil, without the forest to remind him of his youth and his father's memory.

Though the prophecy was written in a book, it was not set in stone. A seer was not always correct in the interpretation of nature's warnings. Was it not enough that they were warned? Wasn't it possible that the seer saw more than what nature intended, perhaps saw his own nearing fate beneath the dirt and attributed it to what was necessary for his people?

Rebial believed this was true. He would not bend to the whims of this aging seer. He would not sacrifice his homeland due to a misinterpretation and cower in a cave. If that's what nature truly wanted, then he would show it that its creatures were perhaps greater than it had realized.

Refusing to allow the beauty of his homeland to be ravaged, he would protect it at all costs. Even the cost of his true love. He didn't want to lose Raela, but this he would do if she refused to stay with him.

He would show his reverence by avenging. As a warrior there was no other way to prove his loyalty. What a forest could not do to protect itself, he would do. He vowed to guard it as well as it had taken care of his people all these years.

The trees would become his fellow warriors. He would not let the invaders destroy a forest thousands of years old. He would defeat every one of them. Whoever stepped foot inside his woods and so much as disturbed an insect or a blade of grass, would not be stepping back out.

Not only that, but his ancestors still lurked within its depths. Where would they go once there were no trees to shield them?

It was not the way of the warrior to accept defeat. There was only one path forward for him. And it was not the path that the other tribal members would take, nor his love if she chose to be so misguided. He would dissuade her.

Power surged through him. How could she deny his strength? It was buried deep inside him, like a seed ready to burst. He would grow stronger, just like the forest, by drawing its strength and possessing its aging wisdom until it solidified inside him.

He would reveal his choice to Raela, so she'd have time

to accept their fate and stay beside him. Just because she had recorded the prophecy did not mean she must obey it.

She would stay with him, wouldn't she? Otherwise, what was the point of love if it could so easily abandon someone?

Besides, she loved the forest just as much as he did. The roots of their love had sprouted there. It was raveled inside both of their hearts, a tangled mass that protected their love for each other. Just like the mycelium that could not be seen yet connected everything within the forest. Their ties ran deep.

He would find her and apologize. It was not her fault that her grandfather had a vision, nor that the elders were denying him his warrior status. Beside the forest, she was the only other light in his life, and he refused to give her up so willingly.

CHAPTER FIVE

RAELA DIPPED HER toes in the river surging through the forest, overturning rocks buried in the dirt. Since she had little time left for certain hobbies, she'd decided to spend the day gathering colorful pebbles to make into beads.

If she must live beneath the ground, it would do her spirit well to decorate her travel bag with as much color as she could. Especially since there would soon be a lack of it within her immediate surroundings.

The irony of her situation did not evade her—searching for stones in reaction to soon being trapped inside one. Living the life of a stone herself, waiting for when she would be picked up and set back down to lead a different life.

A stone was all about waiting, for its future relied on either the actions of another or the circumstances of its immediate surroundings. Being jostled so it rolled down a hill or fell into a rift, for example. Sometimes events many miles away could affect the plight of a stone. A storm or a flood could change its whereabouts. Regardless, the journey of a stone was always short-lived.

Perhaps her own remaining moments in which she could exercise free will would be as short as those moments in which a stone actually had something happen to it. The thought was unsettling.

The prophecy was clear that the time spent waiting would be long. It would take ages for the planet to rejuvenate itself. She would be trapped beneath the ground for longer than she cared to fathom. But like a stone, she, too, would once again emerge when the time was appropriate.

The sound of the water rushing past flowed into her ears. Moisture misted across her face. She smiled at the cleansing sensation, pressed her toes again into the water and gently rolled the stones beneath. She scanned the ripples for any bright colors that drew her. She hoped her awl could penetrate whichever pebbles she chose to make into a bead.

Rebial may have to help her. Perhaps now that his dreams of becoming a warrior were dashed, he would have time to do it. Either that or her lover would spend his time sulking. Blaming her for problems that she did not create.

His anger upset her, reminded her of the parting of the river far ahead, for he was quite adept at breaking what should be one choice into two.

She picked up a bead that matched the color of his anger. Perhaps it would even match her own when she was forced to stifle her frustrations. There might be many beneath the ground.

As she stood, she stuffed it into the small bag that dangled from her waist.

She took a breath of fresh air to rid herself of the tainted memory of her and Rebial's last meeting. She scanned the ripples again, saw a bit of turquoise gleaming back at her that would make a fine bead to accompany the red.

To their ancestors, a turquoise bead could symbolize hope, and she needed every bit of hope that she could get.

She bent to pick up the pebble. When she stood again, the image reflected by the water had turned into two figures, and one was not her own reflection staring back. Yet she did not turn to face her lover.

"Here," Rebial said, stooping down after a moment of silence, "take this one."

She turned only slightly to glance at his outstretched hand.

He held a brown rock out to her—common and dull— as if it were a precious gem.

"Why?" she asked, unimpressed by his choice. "It's not much to look at."

"I like it," he said.

"Because you like boring things?" she asked.

"It matches the color of your eyes."

As she gazed at him now, the sincerity in his own eyes was evident, but she would not let him evade his duty to resolve his mistake. One could not move past the things they did to wrong another without admitting their regret.

"You left me alone in the woods at night," she said, her voice wavering like the ripples at their feet. "Prey to any animal that wished to attack me."

"There were no predators nearby to attack you," he responded. "I knew this."

But did he? After all…

"Vandor was nearby. He came to me as I was walking back."

"Vandor would never harm you," Rebial said. "He knows I would make short work of his sagging flesh and weakened bones if he so much as damaged a hair upon your head."

He reached to tuck a wisp of hair behind her ear and

smiled, as if it were natural to talk of violence while being affectionate.

Her expression must have told him otherwise, for he then said, "I'm sorry. Please forgive me for lashing out at you."

He held the rock out to her again.

"I'm not sure you would deserve it," she replied, but with him so gentle now beside her, she did not wish to dwell on negativity.

They only had so long to be together in these woods. So she took the future bead with a hint of satisfaction brewing in her heart.

"Let it go, Rebial," Raela soothed, running her fingers down his stiff and muscular back. "There is nothing you can do to change their mind."

They'd swam in the river, splashed together in the waves, and now they lounged on the beach. In the distance, rows of shaggy trees framed the water rushing past.

"I will bring them twenty pelts," Rebial said. "They will come in handy in the cave."

"It still won't work."

"Then I will bring them the head of an invader. Prove my right to be a warrior."

Raela shuddered. "I do not like to hear such things."

"Then you can relate to my discontent."

"Of course I can. Do you think I want to retreat with everyone else? Crawl into the dusty ground and never see the sun again? Or at least not for many years."

Rebial dropped his gaze and looked away. He was stewing over something; this she could tell. For Rebial was a product of his passions and thus was not a man to dawdle saying words. Whatever he was about to say must have significance, required strategy in its delivery. Raela had a special love for words. She hoped he would admit that he'd been wrong.

Finally, he mustered his courage and asked, "How would you like to be the wife of a warrior?"

Raela looked at his damp and glistening figure beside her, hair flecked outward, and gave him a teasing smile. "There is no appeal to being the wife of a warrior."

"And why is that?" he replied, a scowl marring his features.

"Always worrying, always wondering whether her husband will come home. What kind of life is that?" she asked.

"If it were our life, it would revolve around love—a love that would overcome all odds of separation and defeat. A love that prevails death."

He spoke in a way that brought the feeling alive within her heart. She turned to hide her blush.

"You would not marry a warrior?" he pressed her.

"I might," she said coyly. "It would depend on if I felt this love of which you speak."

Determination strengthened his features as he cupped the back of her head. Placing his fingers under her chin, he lifted her face and kissed her, successfully projecting his love through his lips. For several long minutes, the kiss continued. Feelings of pleasure coursed over her entire body, and when he pulled away, they were replaced with longing and regret.

He studied her face with a dreamy smile. "I think you feel it."

"But what will it get me?" she asked. "How will I benefit

beneath the ground where there are no enemies for my warrior husband to defend me from?"

Frustration now rimmed his eyes. "You're not understanding."

"Then you need to be clearer," she retorted.

"Will you stay with me?" he asked bluntly. "Above ground so that the sun can beat upon us, and we can make love under the stars?"

Her eyes grew large as she considered this, realizing that he was seriously asking her to do something that would impact the rest of her existence, something that would give her a shorter life just to be with him.

"That way, we could stay together," he added.

"You plan to stay above?" she asked, feeling as if the surrounding trees had crashed down around her. "With or without me?"

"I'm asking you to be my wife if I decide to stay. Above ground, in our homeland."

"Where we will die together?"

"You do not trust me to protect you?"

"How can you ask me to disregard my grandfather and the words I so carefully recorded for him? You know I was born with the mark—the mark of a scribe. What kind of husband would ask this scribe to be his wife when it entails betraying who she is?"

"The kind that thinks her grandfather is foolish."

Raela frowned at him and leaned away. So much for restoring their relationship. Of course, she'd been foolish to think he would regret his viewpoint.

She hurriedly gathered her things, slipped her dress over her head and pulled it down as she stood. "I can't believe you think my grandfather is the one who's foolish," she said.

She cast a glare at his disappointed face before she walked across the sand and left him all alone.

But as she walked home by herself, his words registered in her mind. He truly planned to stay behind. An emptiness grew within her heart as her thoughts raced for a way to change his mind.

All through the rest of the day she stewed, and during the night this anxiety found its way into her dreams. Hazy images tormented her with the lie they would be together upon death. She could not escape them, just like she could not escape him.

CHAPTER SIX

VANDOR LURKED AT the outskirts of the village, watching as the group of men who would never become warriors prepared to leave the village for their early morning hunt. Gathered at the hut that housed their supplies, they slung bows across their backs and slid hunting knives into the leather of their pants. Some distributed dried meat to stuff into pouches. They would be embarking into the woods any moment now, and he planned to do the same, albeit in the opposite direction.

Watching them was the routine way he prepared for his own hunt, for he did not need a weapon. Making sure they went their separate ways was his weapon, for his was a search for knowledge. Unlike them, he wasn't looking for animals to kill. He was looking for those already breathing their last breaths.

And it would be best to avoid those who did not understand his obsession. It would be best to do his studies far enough away so that the fresh morning breeze did not carry his deed over to those who judged him.

At times, Vandor had been known to push an animal on the verge of death over to the other side. Some would call it cruelty—in fact, most members of the tribe did—but he thought he was providing just the right dose of kindness. His nudge was one last caring gesture in an unforgiving world.

After all, why hang onto suffering with the other side so near? An animal could not enjoy its life when it was too sick or frail to move. A human may at least have family members waiting nearby, making the last moments bearable and worth clinging onto a little longer. But an animal was left to die alone, which ultimately led to being torn to shreds by any predator that chanced upon it. Being eaten alive was no rare thing. Therefore, Vandor asked questions that some found uncomfortable. Was a life that couldn't be experienced to the fullest worth living? Why value a life that is failing?

Wouldn't it be more meaningful to take those last moments a dying animal experienced and use them to extend a person's life? Instead of prolonging its last breaths, why not figure out how to trade them for human breaths that could yet be revived? Figure out, even, how an animal's insides worked and interacted, to aid the healers in the act of healing wounds that normally would send someone shortly to their grave.

But of course, to his tribe, Vandor's interest aligned with the dark arts, which meant his meddling was an abomination.

The tribe's misguided perception of him was ironic. For if he enjoyed studying something that was dead, and did it for the purpose of extending life, how was this not admirable? How was this not something to encourage?

He defied nature's wishes, they said, when he studied dead things. If one had no use for the carcass of an animal, it was best to let it rot, let the scavengers come and take from it, as opposed to learning about its insides. This was the circle of life that nature had created. An animal or person should only live as long as nature intended. This had already been determined as the best way, for nature did not need the help of humans to meet its goal of perfection.

Yet nature had also created minds for humans, and the one goal inherent in every person he'd ever known was survival. And wasn't the tribe intent on going underground to ensure just that?

When he'd mentioned it was likely that their own insides matched the ones inside animals, this had only made matters worse. For instead of appreciating this fact, they worried that he was curious about the insides of their own bodies. And while this was true, he was content to keep his studies based on the insides of animals. At least for now, at the advent of his curiosities.

He did not fathom he would ever be so lucky that studying human remains would ever be allowed.

He had not yet tried to study anything that was very much alive, but the thought had crossed his mind. It would be a foolproof way to test things, to introduce death a little earlier to some unsuspecting beast. The spirit world was not such a bad place to be, so was the teaching. But he'd risk the others finding out and lose his place within the tribe. And he'd learned the spirits were protective of their world and did not take kindly to early arrivals, though they hadn't seemed to mind the extra minutes that he'd sent animals there just yet.

Perhaps they hadn't noticed. Such a short span of time could be insignificant to them. If he had to wager, he supposed they might be just as curious as him. The spirits knew they would be joined by all their loved ones eventually. If he prolonged when this would happen, how could they not be interested? But they didn't speak to him as they did to some of the other members of his tribe. And he was too smart to ask for their opinion from the seer whose response might be tainted by the tribe's perspective.

And with the prophecy so close to coming into fruition, that decision he was certain to regret. He did not want to experience the horrors of what the planet would be subjected to—the disease, the poisons, the destruction. He planned to evade all this by going underground with the rest of the tribe.

For while he was curious about death, this did not mean he was ready to meet it. Nor did he want to take his chances and die studying it. One could not promote longevity once death took them. And as for the act of dying, he already knew what to expect. He was quite certain that life would no longer be the focus once one traveled to the other side.

For death was just a word made up by the living. Perhaps what the living called death was just another word for something else.

Even so, all these thoughts did not distract him from the purpose of his studies. While he was yet alive, his obligation to extend life would continue. He'd leave his analysis of the nature of death for when he actually entered the spirit world.

For some reason, he suspected he'd be well-received there.

With a loud whoop of excitement, for this particular group was rather young, the hunters swaggered into the woods. Their behavior caused the females weaving in their circles to stop their activities to watch. All the better for him, so he could slip the other way.

Vandor set out in the opposite direction of the young men. His feet melted into the grass with the ease of a hunter. The breeze moved with instead of against him, and for this, he was thankful.

He wanted to follow the path the prophecy outlined for his people and planned to do so with no reservations. From there, he may just find a new path, an altered path. One where he wouldn't be looked down upon for being curious. Soon he would convince his own small clan to make this separate venture with him.

If anything, he was just disappointed in the timing. He'd come so close to understanding, so close in his studies. Now he'd have to put all that aside for an unfathomable amount of time. Supposedly it would seem like hours in their altered state, but he only saw it as an obstacle to overcome.

His thoughts would fester peevishly with nothing to occupy them. And his mind would grow lazy. Not only was this a waste for the advancement of their species, but it was also one of his greatest fears.

CHAPTER SEVEN

REBIAL AND HIS friends—the group who'd trained with him to become warriors—ventured out into the forest to catch their daily kills. But food was the last thing on his mind. He led his fickle friends deep into the brush, far away from their humble village, to hear his final plea for their support.

Just because they'd told the elders they accepted their fate, did not mean he could not sway them. Perhaps together, they could change the elders' minds. After all, until recently, they had shared his same ambitions.

The location was important because it needed to enhance his speech and remind them of what they were so willing to give up. He sensed this truth to be heavy on each of their minds, for a future warrior could not change his nature so easily. Words could carry weight, but they were no cure all by themselves. They needed to inspire action, and he hoped his words would do so.

When they reached a small clearing, bantering and poking at each other along the way, he narrowed his eyes and spun around to address them.

"Hear me out," he said, already sensing their weariness.

They stared back at him, the playfulness having left their eyes.

"The tribal elders have reduced us to hunters," he said, "but we don't have to accept this fate."

His friends made sideways glances at each other before Devorn, his closest friend, responded.

"There's no shame in hunting for the tribe, providing meals and sustenance for our families," he said.

"No," Rebial replied, "there is no shame in that, but allowing ourselves to be minimized to only that, is much like accepting defeat. And this we have been trained to avoid. A warrior must stand his ground, stay firm, and never back down from a challenge."

"There is no need for warriors beneath the ground," Devorn said, "or hunters for that matter."

"That's right, there's not," Rebial responded, "which is why we should stay above to fight for what we believe in. We must prevent this attack on our homeland."

"The prophecy says—"

"The prophecy only speaks the interpretation of a seer, which means it does not speak for everyone. It certainly does not speak for me."

His friends stared at him, friends who at one time he could rile easily like the bees inside a hive. But an emptiness had infected them, and their passion to protect was dead.

"We missed the time when warriors were necessary," Devorn said.

"I don't believe it," Rebial insisted. "There will always be a reason to defend. There will always be a threat."

"There is no need for warriors when our tribe can live safely down below," Devorn said gently. "And when we reemerge, there will be no threat."

"This is where the seer is misguided. He says our tribe will be transcending to a new way of life. Yet this new way, this glorious transformation, will occur beneath the ground in hiding," Rebial scoffed. "Why does no one see the fallacy in this? I suspect it is the seer who has become outdated, as opposed to that of the warrior. The true threat to us is believing in the seer's nonsense."

His friends said nothing for a time, and Rebial thought he may have actually gotten through to at least one of them. Perhaps Devorn, whose forehead creased with worry or maybe even reflection. Someone had to be courageous like himself.

But Devorn merely shook his head and stepped back into the group. "We were told you would try to persuade us," he said. "The elders predicted this."

"And we have decided that you are the one who is misguided and not the seer," said Bensi.

The words stung with such sharpness that Rebial felt as if he'd just emerged from an encounter with a mad hornet's nest instead of the beehive he was accustomed to. But this did not stop the quickness of his mind. His pain quickly turned to anger.

"And I have decided," he said, the words burning on his tongue to be set free, "that you are cowards. All of you."

His friends shook their heads, backing away from him as if he were a sorry beast. This only angered him more, for they were the ones who should feel like lesser beings since they had grown so passive.

And like the lesser beings that they were, their figures shrank as they distanced themselves from him. He watched until they became small like the insects they'd become underground.

His insides deflated, and his heart sank much like the

sun when darkness overtook it. Yet he stood with the same bearing as the trees surrounding him, and so his pride remained.

"That's right, cowards! Slink away from me. Burrow into the ground like animals that wish to hide. I will not stop you. When you sit in silence like a stone, beneath miles upon miles of dirt, don't bother thinking about me and the life I will be living. Or perhaps you should remember what you left behind, a life as opposed to just a passive existence."

His friends trekked deeper into the woods, not bothering to look back at him. Bensi was even adjusting his bow as if he had forgotten the entire conversation already only twenty paces away.

"There is nothing to hunt beneath the soil," Rebial continued to shout. "There won't even be a tale to tell. I refuse to let myself rot there, excited when a bug crawls past. Your life will be as boring as watching dust accumulate at your feet."

Devorn turned now, lagging behind the others but still keeping pace.

"Our lives will consist of staying alive, as opposed to you who chooses to go running into the jaws of death with no one left beside you," he said over his shoulder.

And then the forest hid his friends and they were gone, both physically and as kindred spirits.

His final attempt to sway them had backfired because now he had insulted them, and they probably wouldn't even bother to say goodbye before descending into the planet's womb.

He sank beside a tree and rested his back against the jagged bark. The forest was so peaceful around him—a living entity whose breath was as pure as the morning breeze. How could he ever turn his back on its beauty?

He considered many things as he sat leaning against the trunk. Solitude gave him plenty of space for his thoughts to move freely. Perhaps he would not feel remorse if it became his closest friend.

Leaves rustled nearby, from the breeze, or perhaps not. And he decided to no longer be a sitting target and stood. He began moving at steady pace, in a different direction than his former friends.

As a hunter, he never feared for his safety when he walked lonely in the forest. He carried a wooden spear and a flint knife that could cut swiftly through flesh. But that wasn't why he was unafraid. His skills gave him confidence.

The fact that he could impale a deer from a distance most struggled to clear. Or that he could kill a rabbit with a well-timed dart thrown from a tree branch. He had outsmarted an elk once, even charged a bear that had ventured too close to their village.

The only creatures in the forest that were better hunters than Rebial were the big cats. Though they prowled the surrounding area both day and night, the tribal members only caught sight of these beasts when or if they chose to be seen.

The cougar's appearance was an unnerving experience for any person in the tribe, no matter the hunting ability, for the question arose as to whether the cat was planning to attack. If the animal chose, it could kill quite easily with a swift bite to the neck. There was no need to appear in plain sight and toy with prey.

This truth fed unsettling questions, such as why the animal bothered to do this. Perhaps the creature only wanted to assert its dominance, they'd say, remind the tribal members they shared the forest with powerful beasts.

The prowling cat would watch them cower as it casually

loped past or would even display itself like a proud statue on a rotting trunk. It was not unusual for a tribal member to return to the village in panic and then feel surprised upon realizing they had not been killed and eaten by the vicious animal.

Although there were times when a tribal member did not return at all. Not that encounters or even deaths by them were an everyday occurrence, it was just part of the life the tribe had grown accustomed to, having lived many years within the woods.

Rebial was the only one who searched for the animals, played hide and seek with the cats like they were his friends, stalked them like they were capable of doing to him. For some reason, he seemed to harbor a bit of luck when dealing with the animals.

Perhaps they saw that for a human, he was a fair opponent with skills that matched their own. They respected him and allowed his escape time and time again.

The history of his encounters with them stretched far into the past.

As a small child, he had wandered away from his mother's side and gotten lost in the surrounding woods. She had called out to him for hours upon realizing he was missing, but the trees refused to return her son. Tribal leaders had even sent out a search party to find the young boy. But it wasn't until dusk encroached, time enough for his mischief to have turned fatal, that they found him.

The men who found Rebial said they came upon him playing with two cougar cubs in the hollow of a dead tree that had crashed onto the forest floor. The mother sat licking her pelt nearby. The men had drawn their weapons. But the mother had remained disinterested, so no rescue had been needed.

Rebial had come running. The mother with her cubs had disappeared within seconds, melting into the thicket as if they and the forest were one. The men took the child back to his mother and spread the tale whence they returned.

Rebial did not know what it was that kept the cats from harming him. He had found himself vulnerable many times over the years. He, too, had been capable of piercing one with a spear, or dragging his knife through flesh, but had always refrained.

Although he was a very powerful and adept hunter, there seemed another reason why this game ensued and with no casualties. Rebial did not know what it was, but he knew this reason existed. He had seen it in the eyes of the cats. There was no menace there, no hunger. Just acceptance. He had permission to associate with them. So he did, and thus he learned some of their ways.

Which meant he was more than adequate as a hunter to fight the war within his woods all by himself.

It was his heart that needed company. His lover was too sweet to hold a grudge. Which meant enough time had passed for him to ask the weighted question again.

CHAPTER EIGHT

RAELA SAT OUTSIDE her hut with her mortar and pestle, grinding a plant until it was merely specks of green. Then she ground it some more. Perhaps it was not best to grind in such a way, pounding a plant into nothing, but her temper drove her actions, and this was her outlet of choice.

Taking out her frustration on the plant would save her from expelling it to her mother or her grandfather. She no longer even wished to show her anger to Rebial, though he was the reason for it, since their remaining time together was sparse.

She couldn't believe he would make such a choice, but she also couldn't envision that he wouldn't. For Rebial was truly skilled at being who he was.

Unlike her, who was partially a product of someone else's vision, which she believed with varying intensity depending on the day. And if she ever doubted it too severely, the mark on her thumb convinced her that her grandfather was right.

But Rebial truly was impossible. And thus, she should not waste her emotions on him ever again. Why was it he could invade her thoughts with such ease, pop into her life at his whim, continue to come back to her time and time again when instead he should just let her be?

But no matter how hard she tried, she couldn't keep her thoughts from straying to him. Who knew where he was, though she suspected he was deep within the woods. She imagined him watching her from a distance, as he had done during their first real encounter and many times after.

Oddly enough, her first memories of him were during the same year she had written the prophecy down for her grandfather. Though they'd gone to school sessions together—where they'd learned to read and write—as a young girl, she hadn't much reason to pay attention to him.

He was scrubby, sometimes even rowdy with the other boys, and he hadn't the focus she had with the written word. She had been taught this was her calling and so she took it seriously. Rebial was just there to learn the basics, become merely adequate at reading. His real purpose in life was to protect the tribe and hunt for food.

As they aged—both now approaching adulthood, or perhaps already there—they'd realized that no matter how close they were to each other, the prophecy always hung between them. It was their only matter of contention.

But as it is with youth, the prophecy had always seemed like something far in the future to worry about. The threat it foretold would never come into fruition during their lifetime. So all their arguing about it over the years didn't really matter.

Now that this future had arrived, or perhaps in spite of their relationship, it would tear them apart indefinitely.

What was she to do? This should be a happy time for her. She should be proud of her involvement in the prophecy's creation, but Rebial's twisted viewpoint had mangled her happiness into despair.

So she continued to take her frustrations out on the plant. Grinding it into oblivion was better than taking her temper out on others or even shouting into the depths of the woods, which would only scare the animals and disrespect her ancestors.

Her mother had once told her that she must have a clear mind when she ground a plant into a spice or prepared it as food. Otherwise, her bad energy may enter and render it useless. Remove its nutritional benefits. It may taste bad even.

But this plant inside her mortar was meant for eating, not healing, so Raela felt no shame. Food did not always need to be delicious, perhaps it was not such a bad thing for it to carry the weight of its preparer. Then she could express without words the anguish she was feeling. The others could experience her discontent as they chewed the sour taste of their dinner.

She scraped the remains of the plant, now a spice, into the waiting bowl nearby. Then she picked up the next plant. This particular plant, different from the last, came with a memory—the memory of her first real encounter with Rebial.

One spring day, her mother had sent her for a walk in the woods to find this plant, for it had a great many uses, one being to enhance the taste of their dinner. Eager for her hunger to be satisfied with its delectable flavor, she had grabbed her satchel and ventured away from their village to search for it.

The trees blocked most of the sunlight once she moved into their midst. The air cooled, and she tightened her shawl around her shoulders. She walked lightly through the undergrowth as she had been taught, out of respect for the animals that lived there. The forest was not a place for heavy stomping, for it contained countless forms of life with different purposes.

Even after many years of living inside the woods, they still did not know the uses of every plant. Walking without care might damage one that, if not useful for the tribe, may be useful for another form of life. Each thing growing was integral to the sustainability of something else. One who did not move carefully did not belong inside the forest.

Sensing that someone was following her, she paid the slight rustling sound no heed. There were eyes everywhere—on birds and insects and creatures all making a point not to be seen—so it was normal to feel like one was being watched. Even their ancestors peered out at them from the spirit world from time to time.

She looked for a specific tree, like the one her mother had described, for near its base was where the plant usually grew. Her mother had told her the tree and the plant had a symbiotic relationship, benefited from the closeness, and she had nodded as a ten-year-old child did when being taught something they were not quite old enough to fully understand.

The tree she searched for grew in a thick grove in the distance, and she confirmed it was the right one as she neared. It had the scaly bark that matched the picture in her head, the knowledge she possessed of the shape of its cone. Reaching it, she pawed through the undergrowth to search for the plant growing near the base of its trunk.

This was when she heard a louder sound behind her, and she quickly stood back up to turn around.

The boy watching her was near her age, perhaps a bit older, with shoulder-length dark hair and an insolent expression. Though his insolence did not seem directed at her. That is merely how he looked at the world; this she could tell.

But she also knew this boy hunted with his father and thus would not make noise unless he wished to be discovered.

She frowned at him and waited for him to speak. Finally, he did, though not because he desired to, but because her expression demanded an explanation for his presence.

"You will not find the plant you're seeking there," he dutifully told her.

"Oh no?" she replied, parting the weeds with her foot to see if he was right. "And how do you know which plant I'm looking for?"

"I heard your mother talking to you before you left the village."

Raela did not like this response, for it meant that he was spying on her. "And why is it you were listening?"

"They never grow by that tree," he responded, clearly not interested in answering her question.

"Never?" she responded, wondering how he could actually know that, not to mention why he would be so bold as to ignore her accusation.

"Never." He turned and walked away.

She watched him for a moment, moving casually between the trees as light on his feet as she was. Or perhaps even lighter. "Where are you going?"

"To show you where they grow." He was several tree lengths away from her now, and she bounded behind him to catch up.

"How do you know they never grow there?" she asked.

"I know all kinds of things," he answered simply. "The forest shares its secrets with me."

Raela had never heard anyone refer to the forest this way, anyone who wasn't a seer like her grandfather anyway. It was the home of the entire tribe and should not be playing favorites.

"Does it talk to you?" she questioned, following beside him.

"Of course."

Was this boy messing with her?

"What does it say?" she asked.

"The forest doesn't talk in words." He grinned. "I wish it did."

The boy stopped at a pair of spruce partially hidden behind a much larger tree. "Here is where the plant grows."

Raela looked down and sure enough, the plant her mother had instructed her to find was growing there quite successfully.

She knelt and plucked it gently from the soil, careful to leave the roots so it could grow back. Her stomach gurgled quietly so great was her hunger, but she collected as much as she could before standing back up.

"Thank you," she said, but when she looked around, the boy was gone.

And so she'd skipped home with a happy heart, knowing her hunger would soon be filled. Yet now she had a curiosity for the boy that could not be quenched, no matter how much of her dinner she consumed.

She learned, not much later, that his name was Rebial. And he'd made a habit of coming in and out of her life ever since. Within a few years, they were holding hands and sneaking away from the others.

At the age of twelve, they had shared their first kiss high in the treetops. He had presented a gift to her—a special flower—and she'd worn it tucked between wisps of her hair until it'd wilted.

But that was all in the past. And today she was only reminiscing and grinding a plant into nothing. She set the bowl down and sighed.

She looked up then, saw him standing at the edge of the woods, watching her like he always did except with a solemn expression. Was she imagining him there? Was he just a figment of her mind?

Her grip on the pestle loosened, but it was not up to her to bridge the gap he had created.

Yet she did not have a bitter heart, so she would allow his entrance back into her life when he was ready.

He moved closer and extended his arm toward her. She stood and grabbed onto his hand, enjoying the feel of its warmth as he led her away from the village and into the woods.

But even though she walked beside him, heard him whisper a *sorry* into her ears that was heartfelt, somehow she knew that her desire for this man would never be fulfilled, no matter how close they were to each other or whether they shared their deepest thoughts.

Their love caused friction, for it was a never-ending tug of war in which a kiss could inspire pleasure just as surely as it could cause pain.

Still, she would go with him.

CHAPTER NINE

REBIAL DREW RAELA far from the village, deeper into the wilderness than she had ever traveled before. As if that wasn't far enough, he helped her climb one of the tallest trees, its trunk wider than their huts.

The canopy was so compact with vegetation they were able to sit atop it. The greenery stretched in all directions, reminding her of a meadow. Mountain peaks poked up jaggedly in the distance. The sky contained fluffy clouds that drifted casually past. The sun shone with a brilliance she may never see again with such a vantage point.

Looking at her lover as he gazed at the beauty with her, she wondered, could she really leave all this behind?

If this was the life she loved, was Rebial correct in saying that sacrificing happiness for safety was a crime? Besides, if she stayed with him, couldn't they change their minds and retreat within the cave if the need arose? Or if life in the forest became as dangerous as the prophecy foretold?

After all, her grandfather would be the one to lead the people. She had fulfilled her duty of writing it down for him.

But these thoughts were forbidden desires she dare not say aloud, no matter how far they crept upon her tongue.

Instead, she said, "Why have you dragged me all the way up in this tree?"

He patted her hand, traced each of her fingers. "I think you know."

So he was going to make this even more difficult for her than it already was. This did not surprise her.

"I did not come here to guess your thoughts," she said, for she could also play the game of being difficult.

He turned to her then, looked deep into her eyes and said, "It's a shame a face as lovely as yours will spend such lengths within dim shadows, when the sun could brighten it by day, and at night it could glow beneath the moon."

Raela lowered her gaze. "It won't be forever. And I think it's a shame that you will perish all alone."

"Then perhaps we should alleviate both of our troubles and remain in this forest together."

Feeling tricked, Raela said, "Your decision is only part of my troubles."

"Then I will ask you again to be my wife. For if troubles divide you, then you should be allowed the choice to decide which path you'd rather follow."

"Believe me," she said matter-of-factly, "I'd much rather stay above ground with you."

She turned away quickly, knowing she'd said too much. He may yet believe her, and then what would she do? Of course, she was considering it, staying with him, but she did not know if she had it in her to leave the tribal way of life behind. Or let everyone else leave her. It was a sacrifice she was not sure she was willing to make.

"Finally, you say it," Rebial said. "You admit that we belong together."

He kissed her then as if it were decided.

Her heart had decided, but not her mind. Yet she had no desire to wither beneath the soil. Above, she could thrive with her lover. And even if they died together prematurely, at least she would die a happy woman.

And they could always change their mind and flee to safety. The future was never set in stone. It was just as malleable as everything else.

It was freeing to know she had a choice. And the choice was hers alone. She felt pleasure knowing he had recognized this, for hadn't she always wanted someone who respected her? She was too old to be commanded by another, practically a woman. And the longer she stared at Rebial, whose fiercely passionate eyes looked at her as if she were one already, she knew the choice that she would make.

"I will stay," she said between kisses. "I will stay behind with you."

Rebial embraced her then, his hands traveling to places on her body that before he had not dared to travel.

And she allowed it, for the sacrifice she would be making was too great to worry about squashing such desires. If her future would only consist of him, there was no longer any reason to abstain.

It was then that she became his wife—the wife of a warrior.

Still flushed from her encounter with Rebial, Raela hurried back to her family's hut. Rebial would make one final plea to the elders while she would broach the subject with her mother. She would only discuss the part of it that pertained to her—the choice she'd made to stay behind.

But when she entered the small confines of the hut, her mother spoke sharply to her.

"Where have you been?" she asked, glancing away from the dish she was preparing. "Your grandfather wishes to speak to you."

Raela paused, her excited breaths steadying as she watched her mother's stiff back. Intent upon her dish, she did not turn and ask her daughter what the hesitation was about.

So now was not the time for this conversation. She was both disappointed and grateful for the escape from the chore that would surely break her mother's heart.

"I will go to him," Raela responded.

She exited the hut and turned to make her way to her grandfather's teepee. He did not live inside a hut like the others but insisted on perpetuating the old ways.

"You wanted to see me, Grandfather?" she called into the sliver of darkness between the thick folds of animal hides hanging in the doorway.

It was the custom to wait to be permitted to enter, even when one was called.

"Yes, granddaughter. Do come in," was his response.

She peered inside. Her grandfather sat on the floor in the middle of the teepee, smoking a pipe. He motioned her inside, giving her a kind glance before turning to stare back at the smoke rising from his pipe. It wafted upward to exit the hole at the apex of the teepee.

He saw his visions when he stared, so he'd told her once. They came to him, soft traces of lines and symbols that merged into pictures, images formed from curling smoke. They arose as mild suggestions that grew stronger as he focused. He had never misinterpreted their signs.

His visions had saved them from hunger as he'd instructed them where to trap the wild beasts whose dwindling numbers had induced starvation one winter. He'd once saved a man from marrying a woman from a savage tribe that had neighbored their hunting lands. His sight had even stopped a woman from cooking a dish with a look-alike plant she'd mistakenly plucked that would have poisoned many families.

His visions had never before now, though, been so crucial to the future of the entire tribe.

Raela entered slowly, careful not to distract him too much, and sat on the soft blanket that also served as his carpet.

"Do you know why I've called you here today?" He turned his head to view her fully, but never did she feel he looked at her outward appearance. Instead he looked inside her, as if he were capable of reading her thoughts or even measuring the depth of her character.

Yet if he were examining the complexities of her mind, he would find no insights there.

"No, Grandfather," she told him, slightly ashamed. Though she shared his gift, so she'd been told, her visions were not as strong as his. They had never solidified and thus were still not real but stayed as wisps of potential within her mind.

He had been looking for someone to pass his legacy to, she knew. Someone he could guide to be the next seer of the tribe. Perhaps he saw his own mortality now within his visions. It was not the type of question that one asked a grandfather.

Still, she wished she could have pleased him by telling him that, yes, she had visions too. This never being the case, she had always known this someone would not be her.

He smiled despite her admission. "Do not be ashamed. I have faith in your potential."

He had always encouraged her despite her failings.

She smiled back. "I fear I don't deserve it."

"Fear is for those who cling to expectations in life that they think they deserve. But that isn't how life works. It guarantees nothing to no one."

Raela just stared at him, not sure of what to say. The many lines carved into his face did not detract from the intelligence radiating from his eyes.

"I have seen the path your future brings. It will bring you joy and also great turmoil. But you must stay loyal to the one most dear to your heart."

Raela straightened. So often, his words were vague, too obscure to understand, required intense contemplation over the course of many days. But today, she knew exactly what he meant. It was as if he could sense the struggle within her, knew she battled her heart every moment of every day since the prophecy's time had come. He must know she wished to forsake the prophecy, that she, herself, had written, to stay behind with her lover.

"I have faith in you, my girl. You were the one born with the mark and thus, you are the prophecy's keeper. It was never meant for me but has been waiting for you to reach maturity. Today you have. This is why I pass it to you now." The seer lifted the book, which had been hidden behind him, and held it out to her.

The design on its cover stole her attention, demanding reverence, but she could not bring herself to breathe or move.

She had been so wrong. And yet, he seemed to have such faith in her intuition.

"Are you certain," she said slowly, "that this task is meant for me?"

"It says so in the book itself," he answered, eyes twinkling. "The book must stay with you so that a generation will not pass. You must remain its keeper until that time has come. It is your duty to your people."

Emotions wrestled inside of her. Her needs and wants were those of one person versus those of an entire tribe. She could not disappoint him despite his false sense of faith in her. One did not refuse a task handed down by a grandfather, especially a task of this significance with such a weighted consequence.

As if she were reaching for a rotting carcass, she held her arms out to receive the prophecy.

He slipped it into her waiting hands. Grasping onto the book that promised longevity to her people, she felt death enter her soul.

"Thank you," she whispered as a tear slid down her face. The book vibrated within her hands, reminding her of its importance.

"You will be its keeper. Make sure it stays protected."

Once she accepted the task, her fate would be decided. There would no longer be a choice to make. Yet she knew what she would choose before the words seeped from her lips.

"I will," she said without conviction.

There was something about her grandfather in combination with the book that she could not refuse.

Yet in two words she had said goodbye to Rebial forever, the one who had just made her his wife.

He gave her a knowing look as if he could read every emotion she was feeling, every reservation that she had. "You are strong. Don't let anyone convince you that you're not."

Then he turned away to stare at curling wisps of smoke, and with one final nod of submission, she stood and left his quarters. She found a quiet place outside the village to cry, staining the book with streams of tears.

It seemed to welcome them, growing larger around her to catch them, as if it, too, understood her pain.

Chapter Ten

BACK AT THE beach resting in the sand, Rebial sifted through the many things upon his mind—his choice to stay behind, his fights with Raela, her decision to stay with him and their act of passion after, even the repeated denial of his warrior status.

Of course, he had tried again. They had denied him.

But even though he felt satisfied with the knowledge that she had decided to stay with him, and cherished their moment of intimacy, his mind reverted back to problems. Perhaps it was because he finally had something pleasant to buffer their effects, but his thoughts settled on something that he'd made every effort to avoid—the memory of his father's passing. It carried a grief that outweighed them all.

His father had not been the only warrior to return from battle, but he had been the only man to come home with his insides showing.

The battle had been over territory. A tribe consorting with humans rumored to be living on barren land far away in great cities was trying to encroach upon the forest. The corrupted tribe had been sent by these other humans to negotiate. But Rebial's tribe, led by his father, did not wish to cooperate with their demands.

It was evident by the ruthless mannerisms of their former enemy, his father had said between dying breaths, that something had changed within their outlook of the world. These warriors had chosen to conform instead of protect their way of life.

The battle had been fierce. His father had hung on, despite suffering fatal wounds, to solidify the win.

Had he relented, then their lands would surely be invaded already, their way of life changed for the worse. Instead, the other tribe had retreated with their numbers reduced to just the few warriors they had left.

And so his father had protected them and made his way back home in time to die in his own dwelling, resting in his bed, with his wife and son beside him.

"They won't be back," his father's voice rasped.

The healer had already attempted treatment with many herbs. Some had been dribbled into his mouth, others applied to the wound itself. Rebial knew that the wound was severe, for it remained wrapped in thick bandaging. It was for the eyes of the healer only, so as to not infect the others with its seriousness—impair their minds with the pain their greatest warrior suffered.

"I'm sure you scared them, Father," Rebial choked out.

He had been told his father may not survive the day or even the hour. And his anger had been overcome by sadness.

"They were only remnants of the great tribe they once were," his father said. "No longer did they act based on their own customs. Their act of war served a god we'd never heard of before, the god of a people who had imposed different customs onto them. Their last warriors died serving not their own traditions but a god that had allowed their quick demise."

Rebial listened, taking all the information in. His mother sniffled in the corner, dabbing her eyes with cloth.

"And they fought differently," he continued hoarsely. "No longer did they stop when wounds were formed, but instead they fought unto the death. They fought until they barely had anyone left to carry the message of the battle home."

Many warriors of their own had returned with his father, some just as broken. Normally the tribes instigated wars that were quick to end when the injuries began adding up. The wars were not intended to kill each other off but served as a threat or warning to stay where one belonged.

"You must not let our tribe be affected too," his father said to him. "You must ward off these people who infect others with their destructive ways. As my successor, you must take on this challenge to protect us."

Rebial nodded his head. "I will, Father."

And so as his father closed his eyes in satisfaction, took one long breath that rattled in his chest and caused a shiver of pain, Rebial knew who had really killed his father.

It may have been the men from the other tribe, but they had been infected with a sickness that his father had warded off. And in doing so, he had suffered a wound too great to recover from.

And to counter this threat, Rebial vowed to fight them and their evil ways unto the death.

For sometimes, it was necessary to match an opponent's strategy. This his father had taught him both in training and now in spirit.

Not even the words of a prophecy written down by his lover could dissuade him. He was thankful she had agreed to turn her back on it to stand beside him. Her support had invigorated his desire to obey his father's wishes. He would not let evil overtake his homeland. He would protect their territory, let the evil transpire elsewhere, but it would not claim what was his. This he would ensure no matter the cost.

Raela's slender figure wove between the trees toward him. He closed his heart to pain and opened it to love as she neared.

She smiled when she caught him watching her, but it was not a smile that brought joy into her eyes. Instead, her smile reeked of sympathy or worry.

"I have something to tell you," she said, placing her hands gently upon his shoulders and sinking down beside him.

But he could tell her eagerness was just an act.

"Then tell me," he replied.

Dread now hovered between them.

"My grandfather says that I'm the keeper of the prophecy," she said, lowering her eyes. "I can no longer stay with you now that I have this duty to our tribe."

Her smile faded as she spoke. Pain tightened the features of her face.

Despite her obvious disdain, he felt betrayed.

"You have given up your choice," he said, standing abruptly. "You did not debate him on the matter."

She quickly stood, tears now in her eyes, and said, "There is nothing to debate. He is the seer. He knows what is best for our people."

"He doesn't even know what is best for you," he bantered back.

"Please, Rebial," she pleaded. "Can't you please accept the prophecy for what it is? As the others have—" she stopped, eyes widening, having realized she'd inadvertently opened a wound that had yet to fully heal.

"You mean my fickle friends, the ones who should be standing beside me? Denouncing their destiny as warriors to placate a weak old man? Or are you referring to the rest of the tribe?"

"Can't you see this is destroying me? I considered staying above with you and agreed to do it. Now I ask that you consider the opposite for me. So that we can stay together. Accept it, please!"

And he did accept it, just not in the way she had hoped. His mind made up, he said, "I will only accept what I can see coming true with my own eyes."

"By then, it may be too late," she replied.

"Too late for what?"

"Too late to join the rest of us. You won't know how to find me."

"That is much my point," he responded. "If I stay above to fight and die, only then will you be correct."

"So only through your death do I get to be correct? You are impossible."

"Impossible to kill, maybe. But my rationale is clear and true. I plan to stay above. Here. In this forest. Our homeland. I will protect it as my father taught me. As the woods themselves deserve."

"What about what I deserve?" she whispered.

"If you choose to leave me behind, then you will get it," he said, turning his back on her.

"I can't believe you would do this to me," she said, moving to face him. "Why must you be so stubborn?"

"I cannot betray myself nor these woods to stay loyal to you. That is all."

"I knew you would react like this," she said. "And I know that you are set in your ways. But before we part again in anger, there is something more I have to tell you."

"Yes?" he replied suspiciously.

"My grandfather plans to announce this to the tribe during a time when they had already planned to hold a ceremony."

He felt the slap as if she were delivering it herself. The tribe had only one upcoming event that would have precluded their departure and it had been cancelled. It was as if the tribal elders were intentionally making a mockery of his anger. Replacing the ceremony that should have been his with the designation of her as the prophecy's keeper.

It was the worst thing they could have done. Not only were they depriving him of his birthright, but they were also rubbing hers in his face—the fact that they could not be together due to her duty to the tribe. And if that weren't bad enough, she had agreed to it.

"Unbelievable," he said.

"I think they did this merely to distract you, in hopes you would move on," she said.

"So they think my passion is only a passing whim."

"Stop taking everything so personally. Would it be so terrible to be happy for me?"

But he could tell that the words coming from her mouth were not her own. They belonged to someone else, someone who had tried to convince her they were true. And now she was busy trying to convince him.

It wouldn't work.

"Be happy for you when you're not even happy for yourself?"

He knew his words had struck a chord when her eyelids

fluttered. Tears streamed down her cheeks. "How can I be happy for myself when my lover plans to desert me?"

"How are you being deserted when you are the one walking away?"

Her gaze grew somber and focused. "I cannot give up my duty to our people for one man. You could at least support my choice."

"What choice? You were not asked to perform this task."

"Do you plan to come and wish me well?" she asked angrily now. "Or will you continue sulking in the woods?"

"I have already been uninvited from the event. I will not be there unless it goes on with the same purpose as before."

The silence stretched between them as if to move them even farther apart.

"I could tell you," she said conspiratorially, "the way inside the cave. That way, if you change your mind—"

"I do not wish to hear it."

"But if you change your mind—"

"I will not change my mind," he said. "I guarantee it."

"How will you be able to endure such loneliness? How do you know that you won't miss me and decide to—"

"Don't be offended. But I won't be coming after you."

"Perhaps you will be wounded, no longer able to fight. You would still stay above and die alone?"

"I am not alone inside the forest. And I refuse to die inside a tunnel."

"You act as if you have never been wrong in all your life," she said.

"You act as if I haven't thought this through."

"I just think you will regret your choice."

"And I think the same for you," he said.

But they merely glared, arms crossed, until they tired

of pretending that their hate was directed at each other, as opposed to the circumstances surrounding them. Finally, they engaged in a shaky embrace.

The woods darkened as they stood like this for many hours, their hopes fading in the dusk.

CHAPTER ELEVEN

RAELA STOOD AWKWARDLY in her hut while her mother pulled at her cheeks and smoothed her hair. Today was her day to shine, her mother kept saying proudly, but Raela struggled with her own enthusiasm. It felt like someone else's day. It did not seem like her own.

Her thoughts reverted to the beginning, the reason why such a responsibility fell on her shoulders. She realized then that the true reason for what was happening had started even before she'd written the prophecy down for her grandfather.

Long ago, her grandfather had told her a story that was not about the birth of humanity but about the origin of words.

His great-grandfather had taught that words were not just meant to be expelled from one's mouth but could be written down to symbolize a thought. He insisted the tribe learn to record their words. It was in preparation, he had told them, of a time yet to come.

He'd pointed out that the forest talked to them in pictures. If one were watching, it revealed signals and clues. So they modeled their recording of language on this principle.

Their language grew more refined as time progressed, much like the wood that the grandfathers whittled until their carvings perfectly represented the image they'd intended to convey.

Some of these practiced attempts could be found upon cliff faces or flattened rocks. Subtle traces lingered along the walls inside the caves. These images faded over time as the tribe's experience with words grew.

Eventually, their language evolved to settle gently on the page. This language that was all their own was taught to their children. The seer had insisted it be so.

Now Raela knew why, for a prophecy could not be taken seriously unless one had an appreciation for words. And so the tribe was prepared for when the time came for her to record the prophecy.

There were things she wrote in the prophecy that even she did not quite understand. But the overall arching theme was clear. Death and destruction would be coming to their forest at the hands of humans similar to them yet different, humans that overvalued their own sense of worth. This attitude would prompt them to consume faster than the planet could provide, which would ruin the environment. Thus the tribe would need to escape within a cave to sustain their way of life, their reward for maintaining a thoughtful reverence for their surroundings.

A time would come when they would be allowed to reemerge into a fully recovered world. Only the prophecy's keeper could determine when this time would be, leading them back above ground based on the map provided in the book. Raela had always assumed this would be her grandfather since he was the seer who the prophecy had spoken to inside a vision.

Sometimes it seemed the prophecy meant something different than what it had so plainly stated before. So it was with words that could be shaped or misshaped, their meanings altered by what words were placed around them. Sometimes words expressed complex things difficult to comprehend. Sometimes their meanings could even change over time.

But her grandfather was adamant that the words so vaguely describing the prophecy's keeper pertained to her. And since he had the sight and she did not, she knew he must be right. It was his assumption she had known all along this was her calling, but this was incorrect. For she'd always seen her future as one that ended with Rebial.

Raela did not have the same gift as her grandfather. No matter how he insisted that she did, she felt only traces of things to come, not complete visions. For some reason, the gift evaded her, perhaps because of her involvement with the prophecy. The fates may have decided that one purpose was enough.

She did not know how she would follow in his footsteps to be the next seer. Especially when she must live out most of her life underground where the spirits of the forest would not whisper suggestions in her direction.

Yet somehow, she would know when the time would come to reemerge. She wondered what could possibly happen to make her aware, supposed this knowing would consist of merely her internal sight and this alone. And this is exactly what bothered her.

A seer was supposed to have the focus to notice when the signs were speaking to them. But her own thoughts were consumed by the worry of what would happen to her and Rebial. She did not consider herself a viable person to take on this task with her thoughts so otherwise consumed.

She was not as duty driven. Although she intended to do what her grandfather said nature expected of her, her heart was not fully into the task. Her heart instead revolved around regret and the fading passions with her lover.

Which meant she was getting ready for a ceremony that she was not excited to attend. Plumping her hair and primping her clothes for a task in which she had no passion.

Her mother pinched her cheeks one last time, draped a beaded necklace around her neck. After one final look of approval, she pulled the animal skins away from the doorway. The sun peeked in, perpetuating the lie that all would be well once she stepped outside the hut.

So with a stoic expression Raela moved into the light and joined the others down the way within the village center. Her mother followed behind, chattering words of encouragement that only succeeded in becoming background noise amid her cluttered thoughts.

Upon her approach, her grandfather gave her a look that said he knew all the secrets in her mind. But he most assuredly did not. And for the first time she thought to question his insight. Perhaps Rebial was right that his skills were fading. But her spirit was too beaten down to dwell on such a thing.

As she stood before the tribe, looks of confusion creased their faces. Some whispered to each other, wondering why she had prepared herself in this manner for her grandfather's speech. He did not leave them wondering for long.

"Many of you have assumed that the old seer standing before you is the keeper of the prophecy, since it came to me upon a vision, but you were wrong. I was only keeping it safe until its true keeper was ready to take on the task."

There were mumbles of surprise now.

"This young woman who stands before you," her grandfather said, "is the keeper of the prophecy as mentioned in the book. She was chosen to write its words, but her duty does not end there. She is the one who will lead us underground. She is also the one who will lead our people back above ground when nature decides that it is safe to return. Only she will know when it is time."

Raela stood before the tribe, her grandfather's words torturing her soul. It was difficult to maintain the expression of someone who was pleased. She may have succeeded.

Rebial watched from somewhere in the woods—she knew this—shielded by vegetation, refusing to show his face but unable to refrain from watching the ceremony that should have designated him a warrior. Unable to refrain from watching her like he had always done.

How could he give up this habit for eternity by staying behind?

Murmurs from the tribe drew her attention away from her thoughts. As she'd foreseen, some seemed accepting of this development. Others skeptical.

"She is only a young woman," an elderly woman said. "How do we know her heart is in the right place for this task?"

Raela cringed, knowing the woman had a valid point. But her grandfather had an answer for everything.

"Are you questioning the grand design of nature's plans?" he asked.

The woman shrank back and shook her head. "I would never question such a thing."

"Raela will do her duty exactly how nature has planned. You must remember I am not the one who chose her. It is nature who has given her this greatest honor. I only relay its messages to you. And this is what it has told me."

"If this is nature's decision, then we will stand by it, and welcome her as our leader," a man said.

Raela scanned the tree canopies overhead, hoping now that Rebial was not watching. For he was supposed to be their leader. Not her. And she did not wish to add any more strife to the mere moments she had left to be with him.

"And so now that we have all accepted nature's plans, I shall present to her the book. To do with it as nature intends."

He had reclaimed the book before the ceremony. And so he handed it to her again, and she took it just as tentatively as before.

"I will guard it with my life," she said with as much enthusiasm as she could muster.

The book's energy resonated in her hands, kept her upright when she would rather crumble into the dirt.

"I accept this task that nature has chosen for me," she said more strongly now, drawing energy from the book. "It is mine and mine alone. I will not fail in my delivery of it."

The people cheered around her, but even as she said it, she felt a sliver of falsehood inherent in her words. As if their cheers did not align with what they thought they were cheering for. But since she spoke the truth, she attributed this reservation to herself and decided not to project it to those around her.

Staring at the cover now, uncomfortable with and disoriented by the unwanted attention, she watched as its strange symbol slithered in a perpetual coil that had no beginning or end. This design was as complicated as the task before her.

CHAPTER TWELVE

VANDOR STOOD NEAR the edge of a cliff that over-looked the eastern lands from where his branch of the tribe had wandered. His former clansman trickled toward him, calling out greetings he reciprocated. He had requested they meet with him away from the others to discuss the newest development, for he had spent much time dwelling on their future.

Raela's status as the prophecy's keeper would make his plans all the easier to implement, but first, he needed the consent of those that gathered around him.

As their numbers grew, he felt pride so many had both-ered to join him.

Yet why was he so surprised? For his people were more curious than the main tribe. Their joining was a union of two directions—east and west. His former tribe had done so out of necessity, for they weren't fighters but came from a peaceful clan. In the past, they'd lived harmoniously in a wooded area surrounded by inhospitable terrain—deserts and dry, jagged mounds of rock.

But long ago, their seer had sensed encroachment, despite the seclusion of their village and the difficulties of reaching it, and so they had wandered until they'd found their present tribe to commingle with.

Vandor's grandfather had negotiated this unification, and though they had been safer, they had lived a compromised existence ever since, compromised because some of their ways were not looked upon so kindly. Namely, Vandor's desire to study the body for medicinal purposes. For the western tribe only saw him as a man fascinated with death.

He resented this, felt it was his duty to sustain what was left of his former tribe's way of life. Yet even they knew his curiosities traveled a fine line. Still, they humored him, for they saw the value in his habits. They knew it had derived from an incident that had shaken their own forgotten village in a time long past—when the vegetation had grown sick and some of their plants died out and stopped emerging from the soil. A new type of beetle had swarmed the area, seeming to preclude a future invasion.

Without healthy plants, the tribe could not practice their traditional form of medicine. Yet there were plenty of dead animal bodies scattered about to study due to the lack of things to eat. As a young boy, Vandor had been tasked with disposing of the ones closest to the village.

He'd done so, scrawny and starved himself, for the animals they hunted had grown quite sparse in number.

At least they still had fish to eat.

This thought had sustained him as he lugged the rotting bodies that reeked of death to where he'd been instructed. But as he did this chore, he grew most thoughtful, and the task ended up piquing his curiosity in ways no one had foreseen.

This was not long before their seer had the vision that

would set them on their way. If they disobeyed his insight, they'd be next.

But even as they traveled strange and distant lands to reach their current home and the goodwill of the forest, the curiosity remained alive in Vandor's mind. As did his resentment for being so misjudged by the western tribe when his habits became exposed.

So his clan, the tribal members who'd come from the eastern lands peeking at them in the distance, finished gathering around him and waited for him to tell them why he'd called them from the ceremony.

"I fear for us," he began, "for the time of the prophecy has come, which means our lives are in peril."

"How are our lives in peril?" his cousin Biko asked. "The prophecy is supposed to save us."

"Although we were wise to join this western tribe, I do not trust them. We need to maintain our separateness."

"Wouldn't it be better to do the opposite?" Biko countered. "Since we are following the path outlined in their book?"

"That depends," Vandor replied. "Do they realize that we are to be included? Or are we still looked upon as the people from the east, or shall I say, the 'other'?"

"Of course, they plan to include us," Elna replied. "No one has made me feel like an 'other'."

The woman's softly plump body and rosy cheeks matched her demeanor.

"Elna, you are an agreeable soul who makes a fine meat dish. But I have felt this 'otherness' in their judging looks. And will our association, of being from the same former tribe, affect their opinion of you when times get harsh beneath the ground?"

Elna's forehead crinkled with worry. "I do not believe they will."

"I fear they might. For the prophecy speaks not only of the wicked who will remain and die above the ground, but also that nature has chosen a certain group that deserves to persevere.

"What if," Vandor continued, "they remember that we are from the east and decide that we are also wicked and choose to part ways? Or worse yet, leave us behind when we are trapped and weakened underground?"

Members of his clan shifted uncomfortably before him. Biko placed his hands on his young daughter's shoulders.

"We have lived long enough with them in peace," Biko said.

"It has been close to thirty years," said his wife.

"Have we?" Vandor asked. "I am heavily scorned and the rest of you have wavering reputations. I think we need to make plans, prepare for the worst when we reach the underground village. Come up with a plan of defense so that our tribe from the east can repopulate the planet in all directions."

"What do you mean?" Elna's husband asked.

"We need to be prepared to part ways with them if the need arises. And if they continue to rule over us like gods."

"What is your plan?" asked an elderly man who had been friends with his grandfather.

This man's sharpened gaze, so focused on what he had to say, gave him confidence.

"Once we all are weakened underground, on even footing, we will take the prophecy from the scribe. And if this means we must part ways with the others, then they can stay underground, and we will rise back up to the top when the time is right."

"The scribe's lover would never let us take it from her," Elna's husband said. "No matter how much he denies its credibility."

"Rebial is not making the journey with us. Haven't you heard? He believes the seer has misinterpreted it and has decided to stay in the forest. He plans to avenge its defilement and save it from the horrors the prophecy describes."

"There are other warriors in the tribe that will protect her," the man responded.

"What warriors? Have you not seen them? Their souls have already been beaten down by the elders. By the time we reach our underground village, they will be as weak as the rest."

"If Rebial stays here, then it will be easy to take it from her," Biko conceded. "As long as we wait until we reach our final destination in the cave, like you say, so that it will be easier to break away from the others."

"But the prophecy states that only its keeper will know when the time is right," said Elna.

"Then we will make her a member of our tribe," Vandor said, "along with her book."

"I do not like this idea of keeping her captive," Elna's daughter replied, who was close to Raela's age.

"Perhaps she will find peace with us," Vandor replied.

"I would not have it any other way," the young woman replied firmly.

"We can agree on that," Vandor said. "And if they belittle us or show any lack of respect, then we will act. They can stay inside for all of eternity, die there, and we will travel back out when the coast is clear and rise to the heights we were meant to achieve as humans."

He felt like a deity standing on the cliff with the sky as his backdrop and all eyes upon him.

"We can even analyze the prophecy," he said, his speech matching his renewed spirit, "and take from it any powers that we do not possess. It will help us achieve our deepest goals and desires."

Members of his clan stood taller as he spoke, having not felt such a glimmer of hope since they'd learned it was time to venture underground.

"No longer will we be held back by the old ways," he continued. "We can start afresh and do what nature intends for us, which is survive this catastrophe and begin again. As the chosen ones."

Vandor looked at the group of nearly forty people. Somehow, they would have to grow in number. But with some careful planning, they could do it.

"I would cherish the chance," he added softly, "to study something capable of prolonging life."

He had come from a long line of thinkers, as had the people who stood before him. They were all thinkers, the ones who understood the restraints of only taking from nature what it provided. Being passive like this, accepting what was given, was equating themselves to being as helpless as children.

Instead, he and his clan from the east would take a little more and claim what they needed to enhance their own existence like the intelligent humans they were. They would succeed at this, just as they had successfully migrated and ensured the sustainability of their old tribe.

Vandor's motivations surpassed most of his people, for he had been the one who'd been most ridiculed and judged. This had left him with a healthy desire to do all that he could in furthering his goals.

Most of the rest were quiet followers—agreeable, just

happy to be alive—so he had to be the aggressive one. It was his way of making sure that his people would survive. He couldn't rely on only nature and the words inside a book. His mind was too great for that. He planned to elevate what was written to match his ambitions.

And his clan, passive though they were, would stand beside him.

CHAPTER THIRTEEN

SITTING ON A stump in a secluded section of the woods, yet not too far from the village, Raela opened the book.

As she pressed her fingers to its pages, her thoughts roamed free, reaching the wildest corners of her mind.

Scribes were more than just recorders of other people's words, she told herself. They were more than just keepers of prophecy for a tribe. Raela decided as a scribe she had this power to self-determine, that despite her duty, this would be the case forevermore.

The prophecy had been written by her own fingers, and this gave her an advantage. Her ears had been the first receivers of its message, and thus much of it was ingrained within her mind already. The words had followed after, forming easily on the page.

The prophecy consisted of several pages that outlined its teaching. But it also contained a map that would show them how to reach the underground village where they were supposed to stay hidden. In addition, the map showed the way out for when the time came to reemerge. And this is what they understood to be her true purpose as the prophecy's keeper. She would lead them out when nature alerted her it was time to do so, upon a vision she assumed. And so, this duty determined where she would begin.

In case she was separated from the book, she told herself. In case the worst happened, she insisted. In case the map somehow got left behind. No one could fully predict the future, not even her grandfather—especially not herself.

She was only doing what someone in her position who took their duty seriously would do.

She stared at the open map before her, closed her eyes and then imagined it. A picture formed, but not all its paths were clear. She opened her eyes to study for a time and then closed them once again. She did this repeatedly until the map was no longer something external to look at but pictured inside her mind as well.

She envisioned the pathways on the map overlapping with pathways in her brain.

Copying it to a tablet had been an option, but would he still come without the future of the entire tribe resting on his conscience? Would he still come without acknowledging the burden she would carry as well—of being responsible for the entire tribe—the sacrifice she had made to give him this chance to change his mind?

The tribal elders would not be happy that she'd made this choice. This was why it was only safe for her to memorize it, and her alone, in case he took a while to join them. They could not dispose of her then. It would make her needed and relevant. And on the day Rebial brought it to them from the outer world, uplifting them in the darkness of the cave with the book and perilous stories of his adventures, she would tell them she was right.

And if he never came, then her grandfather would be incorrect, for he'd said she would make the right decision.

He had foreseen a future that was possible—his grand-daughter dutifully carrying the prophecy underground for her people—but perhaps he'd missed what ruled her heart. He knew she loved Rebial, but there was also love and duty for her role as a scribe inside her heart as well. He may have overlooked which was more prevalent or assumed she was a follower of tradition and nothing more.

Or perhaps he even knew what she dared not voice aloud. He had foreseen that Rebial would do the right thing and bring the prophecy down to them, and she could have the best of both worlds. He saw this satisfaction in her future.

And so she studied and repeated word for word what was written, strengthening the bonds of those words within her mind. The map superimposed itself into her memory, an image she could refer to at whim. She would study and practice every day to reach her goal. And she would show them that scribes were more than just followers. She had the ability and the right to map her own future.

And though she told herself this was all an imagining, a way of coping with her sorrow, that she would not leave the book behind except for in a dream, she practiced what she intended to do in this dream as if it would come true.

Sitting cross-legged in his hut, Rebial picked up a pale bone fragment from a nearby pile and sharpened its tip. As he worked, he ruminated about the book that had changed his life forever.

He knew the seer was correct in his prediction. His father's teachings aligned with it. The memory of his father's description of these invasive humans was still strong within his mind.

He'd been sitting alone with his father at a fire outside their hut. His father had just returned from a recent scouting of neighboring lands with some of the others, something they did to ensure their territory remained safe.

Their tribe had already merged with one forced to evacuate their home. It had been a careful negotiation, for the eastern tribe had told tales of a diseased wood. The plants and animals had begun dying out. But the forest they had lived in was smaller and less abundant than the one Rebial's tribe lived in, which still flourished around them. For the time being, at least, they were safe.

Still, his father had looked troubled as he stoked the fire.

"Father, what is it?" he'd asked.

He could see it in the way his father twisted his face, that he was unsure whether he should reveal anything to him.

But Rebial stayed attentive as if he deserved the information. His father needed to know that he was old enough to hear the truth.

"Son, today you are just a child, but someday you will be a great warrior. So I will tell you the story of what is bothering me."

Rebial smiled inside himself and eagerly leaned in close, keeping his expression stiff and severe.

"When we neared the edge of our lands, where our enemies usually wait, we searched for any signs of them—their tracks, their scent—but they were nowhere in sight."

His father looked perplexed, though Rebial thought he might have the answer.

"They were hiding," he suggested. "Last time you met, you gave them something extra to fear."

He'd heard the story, how two of the other tribe's greatest warriors had been badly wounded. This had triggered the war to end, for the point was not to destroy but to protect. And wounding the other side made the point quite clear of who was dominant, or at least that the threat was not worth antagonizing.

His father looked over at him, though his expression was not assenting.

"That is not the way the tribal balance works," he said. "Warriors do not hide indefinitely from each other, especially when his territory is nearly being invaded. He always makes himself known at some point. Otherwise, he may as well hand his lands over as a gift to anyone nearing the edges."

Rebial knew his own childish limitations, that he was missing something more important, something his father did not wish to come right out and say.

"Where were they?" he asked.

"When their warriors did not come, we approached their village to make sure that all was well. If we were to hunt their game, or if they'd decided to allow it, then we would offer them a bit of thanks, find out why the change in habit."

His father's expression grew more worried.

"What did they say when you approached them?" Rebial asked.

"Their village was deserted," his father said.

Rebial envisioned their own village, empty and deserted. It would be a strange and disturbing sight for a place once so full of activity and life to be vacated—like the entire tribe had turned into a ghost.

And he shivered, because he knew this childish memory would come into fruition for his current self sometime soon.

"So they were hiding?" he asked, confused.

"Perhaps," his father relented, "but not from us. For it was obvious they hadn't been there for some time."

"Then from who?" he'd asked, trying to imagine someone who could be scarier than his own father.

"There is no way of knowing," his father said. "But there are tales of a people who are spreading across the land faster than it can provide for them. Perhaps it was them they hid from."

Rebial tried to wrap his brain around this concept. The forest was his own tribe's livelihood. He could not imagine chopping down every tree for wood, hunting every animal to eat like gluttons, or picking every plant for its herbal use. He could not imagine his surroundings to be so empty.

For the forest to thrive, one had to be careful not to take too much. This was how one showed not only respect but an understanding of how nature worked.

"Or even worse," his father said regretfully, "they may have joined forces with them."

A sickness formed in his gut. For how disgusting it would be to sacrifice one's honor to accommodate this different type of human.

"How will we figure out what happened to them?" he asked.

"We'll find out eventually," his father said matter-of-factly. "The forest reveals its secrets over time."

And so this is how Rebial knew that the seer was correct. But he did not want to be like this other tribe and run and hide. He remembered the look upon his father's face at the mere suggestion—the disgust, the regret, and even shame—for though they warred against each other, another tribe was not so different from themselves.

And if these other humans truly were so terrible and could not understand the ways of nature, then Rebial would use the ways of nature to outsmart them.

Which was why he would be setting traps. Putting brush over holes with wooden spikes in them. Sharpening bone fragments he would mount onto his spears. He would make the village impenetrable.

Inside his mind, he carefully mapped the spots where he would put them, strategically placing them in areas in the brush that would seem a friendlier way to travel. He knew every spot within his woods by heart. And he would make every moment of their time inside his forest a moment in which they would regret their trespass. He planned to make their regret match the anger boiling in his heart.

CHAPTER FOURTEEN

THE TREETOPS WERE now Raela and Rebial's favorite place, for what other area could match the heights they experienced during their moments of intimacy?

"You will come with me," she coaxed as she snuggled against his warm, sturdy chest.

He stirred but did not answer. His hand stroked the hair lining her face. The birds swooped in and out of the tree canopy around them.

"I cannot fathom a life without you," she continued, "and I've always thought you felt the same."

"Yes," he agreed softly. "I cannot fathom it."

"So you will come?" she tilted her head so her wide brown eyes could study him.

His expression only hardened upon her scrutiny. "I won't make promises I can't keep."

She sat up in a hurry, disturbing their perch on the thick branch. She would have fallen over the side had Rebial not grabbed onto her waist and pressed her against him.

"You keep me safe so that you can hurt me later," she accused, untangling herself from his clutches to move away more carefully this time.

"I keep you safe because I care for you, and it's in my nature to protect. Just like it's the nature of this forest to provide for us."

She grabbed her tan dress wedged in a tree knot and yanked it over her head. "Yet you don't care enough to come with me." She pulled her dress down and around her body.

"Must we fight this fight again?" he asked as she smoothed her mussed hair. "I come from the warrior line of our tribe. I cannot allow my homeland to be destroyed when it has provided so much for us. I respect it."

"The other prospective warriors are not so loyal."

She dangled this wound over his head as if it would sway him, even though she knew he differed greatly from them and had accepted this.

"They were not bred to lead as I was."

Her mood darkened. "And how would you raise a child of your own during times like this? How would you advise it?"

He gazed at her curiously. "Why does it matter?"

"Because," she snapped, "you think we can just lay together at your whim, and nothing will come of it?"

He pulled her close, though she strove to squirm away. "It is your whim too."

"I know my own desires," she replied as he kissed the top of her head. "They are with you and our people. I could raise a child to do the work I do, but you would be better at teaching him or her to lead. Yet you refuse to come with me."

"What good is it to lead when the destination is not desirable?"

"I am not desirable?" she rubbed her head against his chest.

"Of course you are," he laughed, "that's why we are together now."

"Yet not forever," she pouted.

"Forever is your choice. You know where my loyalties rest."

"It is no longer my choice." Raela stared past him.

"What do you mean? No one can force you away from me against your will. I will kill whoever tries." He pulled her close as if to prove that she was his.

She wriggled away. "I have to be the one to carry the book and lead the people underground. You know this."

Rebial glowered at the reminder. "Is the seer so frail he cannot carry the weight of what he has foreseen?"

"He delegated the task to me. There must be a reason," she said, although she didn't believe it.

"Surely it's to punish me. And he's using you to do it."

"So you're saying that I don't deserve this task?" she asked, agitated once again.

Rebial stared at her for a long moment. "I'm saying that you deserve more."

"I deserve independence in whichever way I see fit."

"Then perhaps you are a leader after all."

"I'd be a better one with you," she said.

"That's not possible if you choose to obey your grandfather's wishes."

"I was born into a family of scribes," she said slowly. "I was born with the mark. I have a responsibility to our people."

"And I have a responsibility to the tribe as well," he replied. "And more specifically to this forest. One I cannot turn my back on."

"But your family is leaving with the rest of us. And you were not designated a warrior by the tribal elders."

Rebial threw a hand up in annoyance. "I can't believe you would bring that up. I deserve it and you know it."

"Yes, you do. But that doesn't mean you can't be humble and abide by nature's wishes."

"Nature wouldn't waste a man like me."

"Listen to you, so full of yourself," Raela scoffed. "And you will end up all alone, destroyed by the invaders."

"They do not get to decide when I will perish. Only I decide. I promise you."

"I won't be here to see that promise." The sadness in her voice spoke for both of them, she was certain.

"Perhaps the tribe will see the folly of their ways and come back."

"I have memorized every single word of the prophecy. We will not be coming back while you are still alive. I promise you that."

"Then all is truly lost between us. Unless…" Rebial replied, his unspoken words enlivening a devious look on his face.

"Unless what?" she asked.

Sensing something peculiar was about to happen, and feeling unsettled, she swung down then from the tree. He swung down after her.

Now on even ground, they stared at each other.

"It's in our power to alter things a bit," he said.

Raela moved near the book she had slid beneath roots. "The book is what is powerful."

"Yet what your grandfather thinks it says will never come to be," he challenged.

"You mock me?" she asked.

"I would never mock you," he replied.

"But if it does?"

"Then I will be the victor."

"We can't stay married if you stay here," she said, the words bitter on her tongue.

"You are correct," he told her, drawing a knife from his pants. "It would be futile for us to stay married." He stepped closer and smiled mischievously. "Yet I'll ensure right now that you will never forget me."

"What are you doing?" she asked in a hushed voice, wondering whether she should be afraid.

He laughed, grabbed her hand, and drew blood inside her palm with a swift flick of his wrist. "I am linking you to me."

She cradled her hand, pain tingling from her palm, and watched him cut into his palm in the same manner.

Then he held out his bloodied hand to her. They pressed their palms together and kissed each other fiercely.

"Is this black magic?" she asked when their lips parted.

"No, it's love magic," he replied. "It is a stronger bond than marriage."

"So now we are linked," she said. "What keeps our bond sacred?"

"We do," he told her.

"No." She shook her head. "What keeps it from harm?"

"I do," he said, but she was no fool about the false security of pride.

"You are only a man," she told him, and he frowned slightly.

"We need to involve something more powerful if our love is to truly transcend the banalities of death." And then Raela remembered something.

She squeezed his hand, causing him to jerk with surprise, and felt the sting of their blood mingling in her palm. Then she released him, and while he glared at her and backed away, she dipped her opposing thumb that bore her birthmark within the blood puddled in her palm.

She picked up the prophecy from where it nestled in the roots. Rebial's frown transformed into a scowl. Opening the book, she pressed her thumb onto one of its pages. When she removed it, their blood displayed a perfect representation of her mark—the mark of the scribe.

"There," she said, smiling brightly, "now our love truly cannot die."

"And why is that?" he asked suspiciously.

"You forget," she told him, "that the prophecy holds power. It will preserve our love for eternity."

"If you believe in such things. Which I don't."

"Belief has nothing on eternity. If the prophecy can ensure that not one generation will pass if it remains secured within the tribe, then it can surely make it so our love will never die."

"Our love will stay preserved then," he said, "as if we needed help with that."

She tucked the book inside her gown, feeling its power vibrating against her skin.

Then Rebial turned to kiss her and helped her climb back up into the tree.

CHAPTER FIFTEEN

THE CHANGES HAPPENED gradually. Just as the prophecy forewarned, it began with fitful shifts in the weather. Its temperament was unsettled, sporadic, as if it could not decide from day to day which way to manifest.

When it rained, the drops did not fall lightly, but instead came down in torrential sheets as if the sky unleashed them all at once. After lengthy periods of this, the rain stopped altogether and the days grew warmer, so hot that the tribe had to be careful with their cooking fires and even when they lit a pipe. They could see how fragile the undergrowth was, how susceptible it would be to even just an ash falling.

Some days the heat choked them, shortening their breaths and drying up any motivations that involved movement.

Secrets traveled through the air, wrapped around their ears in subtle whispers too soft to make a sound. Insects they had never seen before buzzed past, taking over the territory of the ones that had thrived so happily within the wood for many years. This was the telltale sign that promised change would come soon after.

Vandor's tribe confirmed this, acted skittish, for they'd experienced it all before.

Certain animals migrated away. Strange new creatures took their place yet didn't stay for long. Every animal that approached gave them a sign to be deciphered. The forest grew imbalanced, only lush now in certain patches as uncertainty grew around them.

They grew accustomed to the inherent knowing they now possessed. Nature plainly exposed the future of their surroundings right before their very eyes. Even the treetops blew in unusual ways. The breeze brought stinging scents that were new inside their woods.

The signs were gradual, revealed themselves little by little, led to the moment something greater to fear would arrive. Some smoked their pipes and stared knowingly at the clouds forming.

Worries heightened as they packed up their belongings and readied themselves for their plight underground. Ambitions wavered as some did as little as possible, merely to ensure they had more time to stare and take in the nature around them. These final moments before their departure were crucial, for they knew they would not see their woods again for many years.

Some even contemplated that they would not see their woods again at all since their route back to the surface would not lead them back the way they'd come.

Yet the tribe was thankful that nature would allow them this longevity. Their reverence for the forest had ensured that nature would provide this kindness back.

Raela divided her time. Half of it she spent studying the book intensely, so devout she was in her duty to her people, they said as they watched her from afar. The other half of her time she spent in the woods with her lover, perhaps still trying to convince him that he needed to come with her.

But the time that Rebial did not spend with her, he spent gathering material for his traps. Plotting. Preparing for a war much different than the one inside his heart.

⁋

The old seer was a living relic of all that had come to pass. He possessed a longevity that was unmatched. His age had far surpassed any other member of the tribe. It had been difficult to watch all his friends and so many elders die out before him, yet he knew their existence could never be erased completely. Their spirits melted in and out of the spirit world, visiting him in hazy moments when he needed clarity, even calling him to join them. He felt as if his own blood, or something inside himself, contained a record of each individual, that death had only captured the bodies they had dragged along their entire lives.

The progeny he'd had a hand in procreating were still very much alive, but except for Raela, he kept his distance. There was no need to revere his descendants when he felt paternal instincts for every remaining member of the tribe, as though they were all his children. As an elder, he felt this was only appropriate.

He would focus on the one who would uphold all the rest. She would not fail to do what nature needed from her. He knew this deep inside himself.

The others had long forgotten his age, and it was a sign of disrespect to ask. Occasionally, the very young could not resist the temptation and would bashfully inquire. The old man would just wink and say he was as old as the number of wrinkles on his skin. The child would stare in wonderment, begin to count them, until he or she was led away by an ashamed parent.

The years had wizened him. His cunning mind was not analogous to what his body had become. He was as sharp as the best of them, even keener than some of the fresh-faced youths primed to become eventual leaders within the tribe. He felt the shift occurring despite this. The tribe was in the process of changing its system of government. The young would soon be ruling the old.

The seer knew they would never fully break away from the old way of doing things, no matter how much they aspired. No matter how long they spent underground, they would reemerge revived.

He spent his days staring reflectively into the distance, barely ever moved from where he sat. The stem of a pipe grazed his lips while he watched its smoke move shapes across the horizon. For many years, this union of breath and herb had created images for him, which foreshadowed events to come.

Realizations wafted over him as gently as the smoke floated away during this practice. Still, he pondered whether knowing the future was as beneficial as having a firm grasp on the present. What happens next is always reliant on what is happening now, after all.

Although he had been the one to have the premonition many years ago, had even spoken it as prophecy to his granddaughter who had written the contents down inside the book to preserve its meaning, he knew he could not make the venture with the rest of them. His body was weak and tired. The fight in him was gone, at least in a physical sense. He mused that perhaps there was another way to continue life, one different than what he had foreseen. The power in his brain was larger than what he possessed in any limb.

When a solemn few approached, he knew the time had

come for them, and for himself. They were astounded when he only shook his head, spurning their offers for aid. He would not be attended to. Instead, he steered them away, told them his destiny differed from theirs. Respectfully, they let him be and walked away bewildered. Their whispers revisited him after they had left, traveled back to where he sat and tickled his ears.

They thought he was going somewhere private to die. Accepted it without question, decided not to tell the grand-daughter so her despair would not disturb her role as keeper of the book. Dying by oneself in the woods had been an old custom still followed by a certain few. It was not hard to believe the old seer would follow the same path as his ancestors. It was a well-known fact that the oldest member of the tribe had not conformed to the new way of doing things.

He planned to slip away in the dead of night before they had a chance to return and plead for him to reconsider.

But this is your prophecy. How can you deny what you yourself conceived?

The unspoken words plagued him, but nonetheless, with great effort, he stood. His legs were frail and wobbled as he placed his weight upon them. With small yet decisive steps, he exited his teepee and crept unsteadily toward the spot where he knew he must venture.

It took him half the night to complete his journey. He made multiple stops along the way to rest and catch his rasping breath. Several times he slumped heavily against a tree and remained indifferent when his body became the target for crawling bugs and itchy leaves. It was useless to acknowledge these fleeting nuisances, so he refrained.

When he reached his destination, he paused to view its splendor. The lookout point was one he had enjoyed numerous times throughout his life. What he saw before him stretched out so far that he felt limitless. It was then he knew for certain he had made the right choice and wasted no time fulfilling what he had come to do.

He allowed his mind to expand until what was inside broke free from the constraints. The pieces shot out, in various directions, and soared away from the body that had for so long bound them to the mundane. Each bit took on a new life. He was no longer a man but a catalyst for an esoteric existence that even he did not fully understand. The fragments branched farther and farther away before finally settling somewhere amongst the stars.

❧

The ground trembled ominously beneath their feet. The impact was enough to shake the very legs they stood on. It vibrated up through their bodies and clamored ruthlessly inside their skulls. This spurred a recognition within them that had been long in coming.

It was time.

Soon this sensation was accompanied by a steady sound that mimicked the rhythmic beating of a drum. It echoed toward them from the distance, taking the time to ricochet off splintered wood and leaves before reverberating into their ears. The noise was instrumental in motivating them to expedite their efforts. It was crucial for them to advance quicker than the impending crescendo.

Members of the tribe moved quickly, gathered their remaining belongings into animal skin pouches and beaded travel bags. Children were retrieved and final meals were consumed. Voices murmured between the cracks of the hustle and bustle, whispers betraying the onslaught of *him*.

His footsteps preceded him. Each one denoted his intention with clarity. They were forceful, pounded heavily upon the planet, and no doubt crushed everything that grew in his path.

No one knew who this visitor was that approached so earnestly. What mattered wasn't who he was, but that he was coming. He was coming, and though he would also leave today, he essentially would never leave. His presence would linger longer than he was welcome, and he would end up owning everything that had been rightfully theirs for thousands of years. Without asking or buying, he would not only take it away, but also proceed to destroy it. And in doing so, he would also destroy them.

His arrival would complete the prophecy, for his presence signaled its final warning. He came as one but symbolized the presence of millions. Billions. He wasn't even the same type of human as the tribal members. He symbolized an idea, a lifestyle, a threat. Contact was to be avoided. Even his breath was like a disease. He would not stay long today but would return in numbers.

It didn't matter. They would be gone.

They gathered together at the cave, gave each other looks of encouragement, before plunging themselves and what they could carry of their entire culture into the chasm designated as their means of escape by the prophecy long ago. Brushed with leafy vegetation and laced with craggy edging, it blended in so well with its surroundings that to the untrained eye, it was virtually invisible.

The invaders would never see it with their blindness. Since one could not own or possess a hole, they would not even be searching for such things, would never know its value as the doorway to survival.

Though there were miles upon miles of tunnels beneath the ground, and different openings hidden throughout the planet to reach them, the path of the tribe would be safe. This the prophecy had stated within its pages, as long as they followed the map it had provided. If they did, then their final destination would remain untouched by others.

They would stay until the scribe directed them to reemerge. The time would seem endless to normal human comprehension, but the prophecy promised to obscure the progression of time for them, make it bearable. As long as the book remained within their possession, protected by the scribe, this would be possible.

And so each person took one last look around themselves at the lushness, inhaled the fresh scent of vegetation, and turned their back on all they'd ever known to crawl inside the planet.

CHAPTER SIXTEEN

DESPERATION SPILLED FROM Raela's eyes. Tears glistened down her cheeks. Her posture reminded Rebial of a forlorn flower.

"Why die fighting when there are other ways to win?" she pleaded.

"Who said anything about dying?" he retorted, acutely aware that his own stature mimicked the towering trees. "But if I do die," he added, "it would be an honor to die protecting my homeland."

This was how they would spend their final minutes together—at a standstill. Yet for her, the time was nearing to break away. And somehow, she had forgotten he was not going with her.

Nevertheless, he had readied himself for this moment.

There was nothing she could do to persuade him. They had spent weeks bantering back and forth, but he had remained unaffected. When her words no longer provoked emotion within him, she resorted to exhibiting her own distress. Tears cascaded down her cheeks as she clung to him. Whimpers intermingled with shallow breaths.

Rebial refrained from looking at her face and ignored

her clenching grip. He would not allow her sorrow to infect him. He loved her, but this love was no match for what he was prepared to defend. He stood strong with his bone spear and flint knife dangling from his sides.

"Regression is wise in times like this," she said, her words coming forth as a choked whisper. "I can't believe you would choose ignorance."

"You call it ignorance," he replied. "I call it courage."

He had known the time would come for them to part paths. It had been her decision. She had chosen the easy path, and he had picked the one most obvious to a man of his physical prowess. He was ready. While the others planned retreat, he plotted to avenge. The power to sense what was happening in their woods had come easily enough. It did not make sense to give them so much and expect so little.

"Your denial of the prophecy is denying our love," she said. "How am I to believe anything you ever said was real?"

Weeks ago, she had told him she understood. Her words spoke differently now during their final encounter.

"Unlike you," he replied, "I meant everything I said."

Her face twisted with the recognition that he was correct. "I will never be the same again," she whispered. "I will never forgive you for this."

Her words were cruel, yet she buried her face in his chest, shook with sobs. He wrapped his arms around her trembling form.

Her sadness strengthened him. Made him stand bolder, appear larger, consume deep breaths of air with vigor. The planet sent boosts of energy, empowering him from the feet up. He felt as vibrant as his surroundings with her clinging onto him. Her gesture of weakness would not win even a quiver from his limbs.

Someone pulled her. Whispered kind words and led her away. The trunks of large trees quickly hid their silhouettes. He felt a pull but remained indifferent. He had been expecting his heart to feel discomfiting.

But with this stamping down of his emotions came recognition. His revenge must match the sacrifice. And he would make sure with every muscle in his body that it would.

Let the war inside his woods begin.

Vandor stepped into the woods outside their dying village. The few tribespeople who remained now roamed like fretful ghosts, in denial that their former way of life would soon be dead. They made their final rounds as they decided what they couldn't live without and what to leave behind. His bags were packed, having already made these tough decisions, but he did have one final task to undergo before his departure.

He needed to dismantle his traps. What man would do this who did not respect death? If he were as heartless as the others claimed, he'd leave them be without a care for the unlucky animal who ventured into them.

As he neared, his nose told him that he had a visitor in one. In the pursuit to satisfy its own hunger, an animal had made a choice within a few fleeting seconds that instead had ended its own life. The irony did not escape him. As he approached, he wondered if animals could regret their final actions like a human sometimes did.

A rabbit buzzing with flies lay in the trap, recently dead and thus a ripe candidate for his studies, although he did find those just hanging on to be quite useful as well. His spirits lifted at the sight of its pathetic carcass, though he had to remind himself it was too late. Acknowledging this, he forced his curiosity to wither.

He didn't have time to examine the animal and could not bring it with since the others would surely smell the rotting corpse upon his person. So he decided to leave a parting gift to the man who would ensure his plan to overtake the main tribe and confiscate the prophecy would come into fruition. Just like he'd left the rabbit a parting gift—a morsel of goodness that had lured it into the trap—for its time in the forest would soon turn into an even more brutal game of survival. He was saving it the headache.

He released the catch, removed it from the spikes, and lifted it by a leg. Then he headed back to the village through the brush for what would be the last time in many years. Or perhaps forever. Who knew what the area would look like upon their return, if they would even be allowed to return.

The village was already lifeless upon his reentrance. Bare and empty and depressing.

As for Rebial, the recipient of his gift, the first day would be the hardest. And it would certainly be the loneliest at mealtime. So why not leave him something to make his dinner a bit more satisfying? Though it was doubtful the man would be present at his hut, what with his lover readying herself to enter a cave, luck may preserve it from predators until he came back home. And perhaps it would tide him over just long enough to make it too late for him to change his mind.

Vandor could only hope. Although he truly did not care whether or not Rebial survived the day. So without even bothering to look around and see if anyone was left to catch this gesture of kindness, he dropped the dead rabbit by Rebial's hut as he walked past. Then he scooped up his belongings at his soon-to-be abandoned hut and left to join the others. By now, they should be entering the mouth of the cave.

No one could say he was not a thoughtful man for this last act. And if they did, well then, he would not bother reiterating his appreciation for death to deaf ears.

The village was behind him now. He was surprised to find this did not sadden him. Though change was always difficult—especially change of this magnitude—he supposed he might also succeed at leaving behind a repressive way of life.

As he neared the cave, he took one final look at the forest's lush vegetation and breathed its fresh, natural scent one last time. He paused at the entrance, wondering how the air would smell once it was ridden with poison. Would it smell as bad as a rotting corpse? Once all life on the planet died out, he could only assume that it would.

Still, as he entered the bleak cavern, he was curious as to how the air that sustained life could be destroyed so carelessly. Perhaps there would be a silver lining to it, and he would have something to study from the aftereffects once they emerged. He could only hope that nature would be so kind to him.

As they neared the opening to the cave, passing the great tree that grew nearby, Raela held back. Her mother tugged at her arm, but she jerked away.

"Let me be," she snapped. "I only need a moment to myself."

So her mother bowed her head and gave her one sad glance before walking through the cave's entrance without her.

Raela felt very conscious of the vivid patches of green in her surroundings. Flowers bloomed yellow and purple nearby. So inviting, the forest seemed to be suggesting she should stay. She took one tiny step toward the cave but paused again.

Was Rebial watching? Why was he doing this to her?

What had so attracted her to him—his intense passion—was the reason for their parting of paths. It was ruining their future. His arrogance was too brazen to shake, as he discounted not only the prophecy but also her very involvement with it.

The book she'd tucked inside her travel bag was alive with energy. Quite literally bursting from the carefully sewn seams, it sprang out as if to say she had too much to carry. Raela made a feeble effort to shove it back inside.

Its effects overpowered her, as if she hadn't already considered leaving it behind, prepared for it even with staunch commitment. But she'd also told herself this rehearsal had been merely a passing fancy, a form of coping with the inevitable to make her departure more bearable. That she wouldn't obey such foolishness.

The book protruded once again from the bag, grazing her fingers. She stuffed it beneath her other belongings. Others passed by to enter the cave as she stood fumbling. Strangely, they did not speak a word to her. The strap fell over her shoulder, causing the bag to land with a thump near her feet.

She stooped to pick it up, the prophecy now hanging precariously from the opening before she secured it deeper inside.

As she righted herself, her head pounded mercilessly from the anxiety of leaving him behind. And now this—the prophecy itself even seemed as if it wanted to stay.

Her travel bag fell again. The book popped halfway out. Enough was enough. She really did have too much to carry. No one was watching. Another small group scurried past her before vanishing into the cave, and she took her chance swiftly. With a flourish, she tucked the book within the root cave beneath the giant tree.

She stood there momentarily, reveling in this choice. It brought her what could only be described as an unnatural relief. Rebial had not wanted to know the way the tribe was heading. It was his way of avoiding temptation, she was sure, though he insisted otherwise. He had not listened to a word of her directions when she'd tried to impose them, so he had no idea which direction to head, even if he were to enter the cave.

She didn't want him to end up a lost and depraved soul wandering endlessly through tunnels. The thought of this made her shiver.

Leaving the prophecy would give him the chance to come across its pages, regret he had not joined the others at the onset of their journey. He'd figure out how to join them. Most importantly, he would reunite with her. Maybe she would see him yet again.

A light smile graced her face as she kissed the palm of her hand, let it drift slowly in front of her and then down as if to inspire the tears that followed. Then she turned and passed through the craggy aperture to accept her fate.

No one waited for her inside the cave's entrance.

Only a dark tunnel greeted her, and she hesitantly walked through it as if she were nearing a funeral.

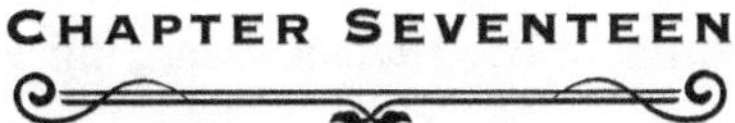

CHAPTER SEVENTEEN

NOW THAT RAELA was gone along with the remainder of the tribe—safely tucked within the cavern, or at least on the way to being so secluded—Rebial decided to scope out the area where the invasion had occurred. He needed to see if anything had been damaged, analyze the imposter's tracks, and look for items left behind.

His heightened senses led him. He took the most direct route, over creeks and through dense tree groves that seemed to open up to welcome his approach.

It was important to evaluate what he was up against, the strengths of these defilers of his homeland, so that he could plan accordingly. He needed to know what to expect, what to look for so he'd recognize their return. The prophecy had been clear this initial invasion was only a precursor to a more deadly one to come.

He moved with the stealth of a big cat, his feet padding lightly on the ground, slinking behind trees and darting quietly between them. The heavy reverberation of careless noises echoed tenuously throughout the wood, and he headed toward these unnatural sounds.

Every branch within his path seemed to direct him. The

vegetation bent to show him the way. The animals spoke in clues that were just as effectual through their actions, scurrying deeper into the woods in the opposite direction of this newfound threat.

Seeing their fear darkened the features on his face and made him move more efficiently. He envisioned Raela's face expressing this same fear. He would not show mercy to anyone who could inflict such a damaging emotion upon another. Even their presence was an abomination, their proximity an insult.

The forest as an entity showed no signs of fear. It quietly listened as it altered itself to point him in the right direction. It appeared indifferent, or perhaps it was expressing a mere acceptance of its future. Either that or it carried the knowledge that with Rebial here, it would suffer less.

It took him several hours to reach the area, but this part of the wood, though miles away, was just as much his home as the other.

When the sounds indicated the invaders were just past a thicket of trees, Rebial moved some leafy ferns aside and peered around a knotty pillar.

The men standing only a short distance away looked like outsiders in their surroundings. No dread coursed through him, for these were not great warriors. Their clothes were plain, easily penetrable with weapons, though made of material Rebial did not recognize. Their feet were contained inside dark, leathery material with an uneven tread that explained their heavy footsteps.

They held no weapons, only flat, rectangular objects and a utensil similar to what Raela used to write. It dangled from the hands of one whose arm was not even extended or taking aim.

They were talking, discussing things in a language Rebial did not understand.

Their voices cut through the natural hum of the wood, which had faded in the vicinity of where they stood. Even the birds weren't chirping.

Yet that's all the men were doing, standing and talking. Rebial's temper wavered with uncertainty as he remembered something his father had said, words of wisdom that now seemed contradictory.

Only when his homeland is under attack does a warrior fight.

The invaders' biggest crime at present, besides being inside his woods, was the stamping down of the undergrowth on which they stood. This behavior, though thoughtless, did not provoke him into action.

In fact, they looked like powerless, pathetic children. Their figures evoked a physicality that could be easily over-taken. They looked soft, as if they'd never had to ration food. This made sense based on his limited knowledge of them—that their most defining quality was their power of consumption.

So he merely stood and watched these men, wondering if they would bring destruction or whether he should wait for a different type of invader—one who actually came across as threatening.

For if these were the men who would wreak such havoc, the prophecy was laughable at best. Or again, its interpreta-tion was not correct.

His warrior friends should have stayed, and together they'd destroy these men. He almost felt guilty knowing how easy it would be to succeed.

Even so, he would evaluate these strange but familiar-looking creatures. Observe them. Make sure they were the ones he should destroy before removing them from his forest. So far, they posed no threat as they pointed out trees during their discussion that Rebial, himself, agreed were worth mentioning to others.

But it was too late to crawl the tunnels searching for Raela and alerting the rest of the tribe that these men were weak and nonthreatening. For even if they believed him, it would take him many hours to reach them and many to return. And by then, what at first had seemed nonthreatening could be inflicting the damage that the prophecy had warned them about.

Even powerless and pathetic children could wreak destruction with their ignorance. Though they were trespassing, he would not initiate a war until the threat became more real.

It was too late to retrieve the others. No matter how weak the threat, his love was gone.

❧

After entering the cave, Raela had crept through the darkness until she'd found the others clustered at the end of the tunnel. They viewed her attentively, some holding torches, and waited patiently for her directions within the dull surroundings.

So she had mustered up what was left of her composure and without making eye contact, she'd told them which tunnel to head into. At first, she had led, but then grief overtook her, and she'd dropped behind.

The temperature gradually cooled as they traversed the tunnels. The path on all sides appeared dingy and bleak. Even more so to Raela, who knew she'd left both Rebial and the prophecy behind. Having decided to do so, she'd not yet considered the repercussions of her actions.

What if he waited days or months to come after them? How would she maintain her lie for such an extended period of time? Where was her grandfather? Had he evaluated her sorry face yet? Would he know what she had done just by looking at her sad expression the next time he laid eyes on her? Would he force her to go back and retrieve it?

For this reason, she would not search for him in the crowd just yet. She'd keep her distance from his deserved position up front by staying a short distance behind the others. Though it was odd he did not seek her out either. How comforting his swift pat upon her back would be, assuring her that all was well even though it most assuredly was not.

But he was wise and perhaps was allowing her time to reorganize her thoughts and adjust to her new situation. He had to have known that she was in love.

Before long, they stopped to rest within an open cavern, and the entire tribe milled about chatting while drinking from casks of water. She did not see him then either as she stood alone, but she also did not look too closely, for he surely would be looking back. And her grandfather would look deeper than she would like.

She did not know how long she could go without telling him. Her only goal was to wait until it was too late to return. Surely with the invaders having already reached their homeland, this would not take long.

As time passed, she became more alert and receptive to those around her, compelling her to notice things. Members of the tribe stared at her discreetly and whispered to each other. She assumed they were gossiping about her having to leave behind the one she loved the most.

As the prophecy's keeper, they probably thought she belonged to them, that she was someone they could evaluate and discuss as if she were an object as opposed to a person. What else could possibly be the reason for their interest?

They'd seem to have long accepted she was the prophecy's keeper. Perhaps they still questioned the legitimacy of her position. Still questioning this herself, and in light of her recent action, she did not blame them.

She also did not bother hiding her anguish. They deserved to know how she felt about her sacrifice to them. Perhaps then they'd treat her kindly when they discovered what she'd done.

After a few more hours of sniffling through the passage, she realized that her grandfather was not just evading her for some wise or thoughtful reason. He truly was missing in every direction she looked and was not recognizable within any of the small groups. Did the pitied looks on the others' faces carry more weight than she'd assumed? Was something else hiding within the crinkles between their eyes, the lines that framed their frowns?

She hurried forward, weaving around person after person, searching for that missing face. But the faces she passed were not the one that she was seeking, and they only turned away.

Finally, she found her mother, whose long face only aggravated the urgency she felt.

"Where is my grandfather?" she asked.

Her mother turned toward her, almost spoke but refrained. She tilted her head as if to console her daughter once again. Cold fingertips lightly touched Raela's arm.

"Your grandfather has passed," her mother said.

Raela knew from her mother's saddened features this was

true. It was not in the older woman's nature to mislead about such things.

Tears spurted from Raela's face and rained down her cheeks. "Where? When?"

"Two days ago. He came up missing. We assumed he left to die alone as his forefathers did. He, himself, was very old." Her mother said all this as if it should bring her comfort.

"How do you know he did not fall ill somewhere, away from the village, or was too injured to come back to us?" Raela asked.

The others parted around them and continued walking.

"They found a body they think was his." Her mother's voice wobbled.

The implications caused a shudder from Raela. Despite how the body may have looked, this woman, her mother, did not even allow her to attend the burial, which had probably been thrown together at a moment's notice since they would so soon have to leave.

How convenient for them that she'd spent the last few days with Rebial.

Her mother pressed her lips together in pity. Raela trembled, but this time with fury. Others from the tribe moved past hurriedly, not wanting to involve themselves in matters more painful than their own plight.

"Why was I not told?" she asked.

Her mother bit her lip. "The elders thought if you found out that you may make a rash decision and refuse to complete your duty to your people."

More anger coursed through her. And resentment. Once again, the choice had been made for her.

"I am not a weapon or a play piece for the tribe," she said. "I deserved to know that my grandfather had passed."

"It was the decision of the elders," her mother said. "But you would be wise not to address it with them today."

Raela said nothing as her mother wrapped an arm around her shoulders.

"Come, let me lead you. You will feel better after a time."

Raela walked numbly beside her mother, who suddenly seemed like a stranger. Was she being helpful for her daughter's sake or the prophecy that she undoubtedly thought Raela carried? How could her mother—someone who supposedly loved her—betray her like this?

"You will feel better once it is your time to lead again," her mother said. "You will find your purpose in that."

Torches that the others carried lit the path before them. They bobbed up and down in what would have been pure darkness.

But the path behind her was more appealing. Raela glanced over her shoulder to gaze longingly at the gloom. It was not too late to rejoin Rebial. After this betrayal, it would be an easy thing to do. But her mother pulled her insistently in a gentle manner, as if she knew what her daughter was thinking.

"You will emerge again," her mother crooned. "We'll all emerge again."

Raela followed silently beside her, a sickness twisting in her gut at the mention of this false comfort. This comfort that the tribe clung to was now in jeopardy because of her.

Guilt and spite battled inside her. The tribe deserved this. But the question remained unanswered for now, what did she, herself, deserve?

CHAPTER EIGHTEEN

AFTER WITNESSING THE invaders depart his woods, Rebial trekked back to the village. The moon's glow was just starting to illuminate the treetops as he neared, and the cricket's whirring crescendo filled his ears. The ground was cool and moist. An unsettling stillness greeted him at the outskirts of the deserted village. It had never been so dark and foreboding upon his approach.

The eerie silence coming from the empty huts filled him with discomfort. Even his dwelling seemed less inviting than usual.

Just outside its dark exterior, he decided to cook himself a simple stew using ingredients he knew he had on hand—plants and broth. He sighed. A meal once satisfying was now an underwhelming chore. After making a fire, he went inside to gather his food.

As he poured his broth into his pot, which he'd left alongside his hut, he noticed that someone had dropped the carcass of a rabbit near his cooking utensils. Miraculously, it still looked fresh. Had it been Raela or Devorn? Even though his friend was the hunter, Vandor was who he thought of whenever he saw a dead animal in unusual places. It was hard to know who would have left it for him.

Raela had never killed a rabbit, Devorn was still mad at him, and Vandor had probably done more questionable things before leaving the village than he wanted to know. And really, it could have been anyone who had not had time to cook it. But he would take the gift, no matter who was the giver, for he would not let such things go to waste.

He skinned it without enthusiasm and added the meat to his pot. The broth bubbled, and he stirred it slowly as it cooked.

Shadows moved nearby, accompanied by subtle rustling sounds, tricking him into thinking someone was approaching. Despite his hopes wavering, he knew he was only hearing the scampering of small animals or the breeze whisking items about. The realization he was vastly alone worsened as time went on. Sounds that before would have remained unheard within the din of supper time now seemed loud against the backdrop of silence.

When the soup's scent told him it was ready, he dipped his clay bowl into the pot and spooned mouthfuls down his throat. As the stew filled his empty stomach, it provided satisfaction after all.

Still, the silence was disarming. The sounds of his own eating filled it. These sounds that had always seemed so minor were now loud and animalistic. He ate slowly to minimize the noise of his own chewing.

Inside his thoughts, something worked its way into his attention like groping fingers, distracting him from his food. Something far off in the distance. Something was there. This knowledge was at first subtle, but the more he acknowledged its existence, the more noticeable it became, strengthening its impact on him.

It poked and prodded, causing him to lower the spoon that neared his lips.

The something that nagged at him was coming from the vicinity near where his people had escaped. Near the cave. Was it Raela having second thoughts? Had she returned? Was she lingering near the cave opening, either too afraid to walk lonely through the night or else hesitant as to whether she should make the final step back into the forest?

His heart filled with happiness as he set his bowl down in the grass.

He would help her make that final step. Not only into the woods but back to his hut where they could bask in the freedom of having a village to themselves. What a difference it would make if there were two instead of one. An abundance of wealth to share was better than having too much for oneself to even care about or want.

He stood and headed toward the cave. An urgency gripped him even tighter as he neared. The noise of insects reduced to a soft hum as he grew closer to what drew him. And whatever it was, or whoever—hopefully Raela—became all the more mentally consuming with each step forward.

The cave's entrance was so obscured now that he could barely see it in the twilight. New vegetation already grew around it or perhaps the last person to enter had camouflaged it from behind. Either way, there was no indication of anyone loitering near the cave's mouth.

He poked his head inside the dark opening to make sure.

"Raela?" he called into it.

A voice echoed back at him. At first, it fooled him into

thinking someone else had responded, but then he realized that the voice was his own.

There was no one nearby. His instincts quickly deduced this as he scanned the surrounding darkness. Yet the feeling that something was present, now opposed to someone, did not recede.

He moved about slowly, examining the surrounding plant life.

A hulking tree captured his attention, growing near a cliff he knew was there, although it was not visible in the dusk. He moved closer to the massive trunk.

It was much larger than the others, with its roots bunched underneath to form a small root cave.

Whatever captured his attention lurked inside. An animal could use it as a lair, but there was no reason to think that a mink or raccoon would be enough to draw him from his supper, as this had never happened before.

What lay inside was powerful, but not so dangerous that it would harm a tree.

He pondered next to the trunk, for some reason refraining from stooping down to look inside.

It was dark. He wouldn't be able to see inside anyway. The moonlight did not reach such places as the root cave beneath a tree. He would have to reach or crawl inside, neither something he wished to do since it did not seem wise to meddle with restricted vision.

Instead, he pressed his palm onto the bark.

A jolt of energy pressed back and sent him stumbling. The tree flashed a blinding light that coursed through its roots into the soil. Its trunk seemed to grow minutely before his eyes, enlivening with vigor.

And suddenly, he knew what rested inside the tree. This

realization lessened the effects of his unusual experience, despite this tree still burgeoning with life before him.

It was the prophecy. She'd left it there to haunt him. Remind him every day of the choice that he had made. Perhaps she had even hoped that he would bring it to her. Hadn't she said that it contained a map?

Anger rose in his chest. His neck grew warm.

Of course, this had been her intention. She had hoped that he would have second thoughts and follow. It was a selfish wish, and he resented her for tempting him.

Yet the tribe was not here, and thus perhaps she'd kept the map. Or memorized it, which she had the capacity to do. Hadn't she studied the prophecy for days on end once she'd known that she was designated its keeper?

He could reach inside the tree and pull it free. Then he would know for sure what she had done. Yet he desisted, not wanting to touch it. His desire for Raela would grow just as solidly as the tree then, and this he could not bear. He'd already been at a tipping point before he'd made this discovery.

But also, hadn't she claimed that the tribe's longevity would depend on remaining in possession of the book? So now, she was making him responsible for the longevity of the tribe. This was an unfair burden—unfair to him and even to her. No one should have this duty resting on their shoulders.

He turned away. Its power vibrated with intensity behind him.

Her selfish act could be perceived in another way, one that would benefit him. Once she realized that he would not follow, she might come back for it. Maybe she had even left it as a marker, a reason to return.

This thought brought him joy, though already the worry crept in that she would come when the forest was no longer a safe place to be. He might be busy avenging many miles away when she returned.

He could move the prophecy to the mouth of the cave so she would not have to exit, but then he'd have to touch it. And this was not a risk he wished to take. This simple act might convince him to do more.

And so he walked away, feeling as if it reached out to dissuade him. Turning back one last time to make sure this was just his imagining, he swore he could see its emblem outlined in the bark for just a moment before it disappeared again—a trickery of the eyes.

Or perhaps the tree itself was judging his retreating figure. Like a solid yet wrinkled old man, it now possessed the personality of the book. And for the rest of the evening, after he'd returned to his deserted village and crawled inside his hut, the pull of the prophecy tormented his soul.

∽

The time came again for Raela to direct everyone inside the cave. Despite the misery that followed her through the tunnels, her mind had been carefully mapping out their whereabouts inside her head.

They waited for her at the bend, having carefully followed her initial instructions. Upon her approach, an elder took one look at her sullen face and spoke.

"Perhaps we should relieve you of your duty as our leader, for you do not look up to the task. Hand over the map."

Raela glared at the man, someone whose kindness before this moment had always seemed out of convenience.

Not to mention he had been the one who had first suggested that they cancel the warrior ceremony. Was he also the one who had decided to keep the secret from her of her grandfather's passing?

But she wasn't so angry as to ignore that her perception may have fallen victim to her despair. She knew this was a stressful time for everyone, and so she softened her expression.

"I will not resign from my duty," she responded. "We will take the left-hand tunnel and proceed from there, keeping left until we reach an open area. There, we shall stop to rest and stay the night."

She did not want to get too far ahead. It would be best if Rebial had time to catch up. Besides, the grandmothers and grandfathers were struggling with the journey. Their pace had slowed to the point that her own dawdling steps were not too far behind. Not to mention the obvious fatigue of those who held small children. The new mothers clutched their babies tightly. Raela knew why—they all did—and did not blame them for being so protective.

"I did not see you consult the map," the elder responded suspiciously.

"Then you weren't watching closely," Raela retorted, moving swiftly past him.

The others followed, and after a while, she allowed herself to fall behind again.

As she straggled behind the elderly, she decided that to maintain the lie she possessed the map, she'd wander off by herself every so often and hunch over, pretending to be staring at it. This would make it easier for her to do the other task she'd decided upon earlier in the day.

Even though Rebial had the prophecy and thus could

deduce the way himself, she wanted to make it even easier on him.

So, every so often, she placed a small bead on the stone ledges jutting from the cave walls to let him know he was on the right path. She'd pluck these beads from her very own travel bag; thus, they should look familiar to him. But she would keep the one that he'd chosen for her that day on the beach, the one he'd claimed matched the brown hue of her eyes.

It could get lonely walking the way alone. She was lonely and yet she traveled with a bevy of others. These beads were a reward for making it so far, a reminder she was the prize at the end of the long dark tunnel.

She dared not patronize the thought that the invaders would decide his fate before he had a chance to change his mind. Though it was a possibility, she knew her Rebial could not be taken down so easily. Not her man who could wrestle with the big cats or toss a spear better than any of the other warriors.

This did not mean the walk through the tunnels would be an easy one by himself. Rebial was used to brush and vegetation, large trunked trees with many branches, not dark stone walls—cold to the touch and hardened like her heart would be if he did not share this existence with her.

CHAPTER NINETEEN

THE NEXT MORNING, Rebial woke to a silence he was unaccustomed to. Yes, the birds were chirping their normal song in sporadic yet melodic bursts, but there was no rustling of movement, no clanging of pots or even the beginning scents of a smoldering fire.

He was truly all alone—an odd sensation. He rolled out of bed and pulled on his pants. He swept aside the animal skins that served as his door and stepped from his hut.

Rays from the sun illuminated his surroundings in patches of light. He half expected to see someone come around the side of their hut, but instead, the stillness matched the silence.

He had no desire to start his day eating another lonely meal by himself in this empty village. There would be time for such things later. Instead, he'd spend his morning setting traps. That way he'd at least have some satisfied thoughts to accompany him when he did decide to eat.

Now that everyone else was gone, it was safe to assemble them, for he did not have to fear someone from the tribe accidentally stepping into one. He only despised their opin-

ions, not the people they were. And now that they were gone, he would not dwell on their shortcomings.

Based on what he'd witnessed the day before—the pathetic invaders retreating for some unknown reason—he did not feel the urgency one should have when their homeland was about to be invaded.

Even the prophecy had stated there would be a span of time after the omen, which had come in the form of unwanted footsteps breaching their land. And he did not deny that it contained insights. The tribe had taken no chances and left immediately, but Rebial knew that he could set his traps at a leisurely pace.

So he set out in the opposite direction of the prophecy since its location was deeper in the forest. It pulled at him within the silence, in some subliminal way he only sensed yet could not quantify with words. He'd plan not to venture toward it at all if he could help it. Not now, not ever. Not unless she came back for it.

His walk down the narrow dirt path that led to where he'd stashed his materials was peaceful. Trees gently wavered overhead and brush tickled his ankles. It was difficult to believe an area so pure and natural would soon be the setting for destruction. But now that this truth neared, he pondered this reality.

He assumed these humans he'd seen the day before, the harmless children that they were, would attempt to move into his woods. They may even try to take over his village, so he'd set many traps around its exterior.

He supposed these men would pick the plants more rapidly than they could grow back, kill animals for food faster than they could reproduce. Perhaps they'd even have the same disgusting habits as his fellow tribesman, Vandor.

The thought caused him to jerk with disdain, as if to rid himself of the thought.

The invaders planned to take over his territory for their own purposes and would live in a way that was imbalanced. This would ruin the forest, though it would be gradual.

The forest would tell the truth—explain its plight—by way of faltering, but one had to be receptive enough to notice. And he knew these humans would not understand. Their lack of respect for nature is what he planned to avenge. This was much the reason he had stayed behind.

Finding his supplies within an old animal den rimmed with brush, he stooped to pick up the wooden spikes, the many lengths of treated vine.

Then he set out to construct his traps around the perimeter of the village. He even ventured into parts of the forest too far away to be their territory, yet he vowed to protect it all the same since no one else would.

And once his traps were set strategically, he would wait for the men's return.

❧

Raela spent an uncomfortable evening in the cave, enclosed within a silence that was occasionally disrupted by snores and whimpers, none of them her own. Finally, the tossing and turning ended when someone declared it must be morning already. After everyone had gathered their composure along with their belongings, she'd directed them into the correct tunnel so they could continue onward.

Feeling particularly weakened by the loss of her grandfather, her lover, and her former way of life, she plodded through the passageways. She hoped that everyone was preoccupied with their own troubles and thus, she could mope and sigh undetected.

Though she soon found herself a short distance behind the others, there was one person whose attention she could not escape.

Much to her disgust, she'd noticed that Vandor had taken a fancy to her. He stayed only just a ways ahead. His eyes followed her along the path. His movements slowed when she neared.

She wished more than anything she could reveal to him she was the wife of a warrior, in hopes this would sully her to him and prompt him to look elsewhere, but to be safe, she bore the brunt of his stares in silence.

When Rebial caught up, she would tell him, and they'd laugh together at Vandor for daring to look twice at his wife.

Of course, presently he did not know that she was the wife of a warrior. No one knew. Raela would have to keep that treasured secret to herself.

Even so, Vandor knew she had just left Rebial behind. He was foolish to think that he could sway or attract her.

Or perhaps the thrill of the hunt provoked him so. He was a man with odd desires.

Just when she thought that she'd rid herself of him, for she no longer saw him lurking at the tunnel bend, he appeared from out of the shadows lining the tunnel.

"Can I give you a hand?" he asked, sneaking up beside her.

"No, thank you," she murmured, not bothering to exert the energy to speak more clearly to such a despicable man.

Vandor did not deserve even a moment of her attention. She hated how his eyes felt upon her skin. How he tried to read her beyond how she wished to portray herself. It differed from the way her grandfather used to look at her—the depth Vandor sought was not to understand but to analyze for his own twisted purposes. A man this uncomfortable to be around only caused one more fatigue.

"Perhaps I could lighten your burden by carrying your heaviest weight? Such as your bag or the prophecy—"

"You cannot have it, Vandor," Raela snapped, drawing the attention of a few others farther up the tunnel.

Vandor held out his hands in deference to her. "I just thought I'd help—"

"You are no help," she said emphatically.

"Such an angry woman you've become," he responded. "Are you certain I cannot do anything to make the journey easier for you?"

Vandor looked at her as if she were a sorry beast, which made her skin prickle. She refused to be his next wounded animal.

"You can stay away," she said, "far, far away. And stop watching me from the shadows, waiting to swoop in like a buzzard."

And with that statement, Raela found her energy returning, and so she brushed past him.

But she sensed him watching as she weaved around the others to distance herself from his trespassing gaze.

Chapter Twenty

REBIAL SOON DISCOVERED that time becomes an odd thing when one lives all alone with only the sun and moon dictating their actions. When you're alone, there is no one to count the days with you, no one to remind you when to eat dinner, no one to tell you it is time to hunt. Although there are preferred times of day to do these things, it is difficult to keep track or even care when you're alone.

Only the needs of his own mind and body now ruled him. He ate only when hunger rattled through his gut. He hunted only when his cupboards were bare. And he slept until his dreams ended.

And with solitude so draining, he slept more than he normally would. He stretched the morning hours so he could fill them with dreams since there was no one to tell him he was being lazy. Mainly these dreams were about Raela, moments they'd shared before she'd left. These hazy moments with her in the dream state he preferred over his waking time alone.

He'd awaken slowly, with a smile spread across his face before reality shaped his awareness into one of bleak acceptance.

Until there came a morning in which his dreams were not so kind. He awoke in a panic, having just emerged from a nightmare in which someone was chopping him apart limb by limb. Thankfully, his limbs were still intact when he awoke, allowing him to bolt upright in terror. But as he struggled to control his breathing, his uneasiness did not subside.

Something awful was happening. Something was suffering as he'd suffered in his dream. Was it an animal?

He rushed to put on his clothes, jamming his legs one by one into his pants. Grabbing his knife, he looped a spear into his trousers and ran out of his hut. Standing outside its entrance, the breeze carried the evil deed to him on invisible wings.

Trees wailed in a subtle horror that rippled toward him. Their shock flowed into him, activating his muscles. A persistent aching in his chest came next, propelling him to move.

Instinctively, he followed the source of the pain, retracing his steps to where the invaders had entered his woods so many days ago now. Cries came not only from the trees, but they also came from his ancestors. They must have been shaken from the spirit world the same way he'd been jolted from his dream. Their spirits hovered with haunted faces, following behind him.

Anger flowed through his veins, and he wished he could infuse it through the roots of the entire forest so the trees could avenge their suffering and these evil men would let them be. But he would have to be the lone avenger.

Many animals fled past him in the opposite direction—elk and deer, rabbit and squirrel—in even more terror than he had witnessed the time before. Birds squawked as they flew overhead.

Sprinting now to where the suffering was being inflicted, he was grateful he'd thought to practice his stride in the days leading up to this. For the war he'd been preparing for had started many miles away from the village. He imagined that his speed would match even the big cats if they were running alongside him.

Even so, his muscles ached, and his heart pounded heavily. He pushed these nuisances aside.

A buzzing sound grew louder as he neared the far reaches of the wood, drowning out the cries of nature though not in totality. The ground trembled beneath him. Soon he would be there to avenge.

But when he burst through the tangled thicket and into the area that he'd envisioned would be rampant with mayhem, the war had already been fought. And the aftereffects of this great assault were more disturbing than he could possibly have imagined. For the attack had left behind an emptiness he was unprepared for.

Death stretched before him—rows and rows of stumps with dust still settling around them. These dead nubs were what remained of his trees, a portion of the forest now wiped out. The great trees that had given gifts to his people, during ceremony and rituals, had been murdered. The trees in which his ancestors were buried lay scattered in the distance, sap oozing like blood from their trunks.

No clear enemy stood nearby. He had to venture farther down a hill, vulnerable and unshielded, before his eyes finally zeroed in on the culprits far away.

Huge, one-armed creatures loomed at the edge of all the death. They were segmented and brightly colored like insects. Strange symbols—black markings—emblazoned their sides. But they were much larger than insects, for their large claws picked trunks up from the ground with ease and stacked them into tidy piles within their upturned shells. These piles reminded Rebial of the heap of bones leftover from one of the last feasts his tribe consumed before their departure.

His muscles bulged as his thoughts turned grim. Veins pulsating, his eyes narrowed. A mighty surge of energy rushed through him, and he found it difficult to stand still as he considered his next move. He knew what he wanted to do—fly with a howl across the rows of stumps and spear the hideous creatures with quick precision.

His plan soon halted when something crawled out of the side of a beast and began climbing in the stacks of logs that once were living. This something resembled a man, though he was dressed somewhat differently than the initial invaders. Yet this man was more deadly, for he could enter and control a beast. How was this possible?

Rebial could only equate his new enemy to a form of parasite he had seen scavenging around in the flesh of wild animals, despite this man, unlike a parasite, being his size. A yellow bowl was clamped atop his head, and dark bands stretched over his shoulders and down his chest. His shirt was colorful in patches, while his pants were a dull blue color. From such a distance, his large and narrow feet reminded him of oval hooves.

As he studied this new specimen of human, more emerged from unseen places. They multiplied like cockroaches, scuttling together to speak amongst themselves. The discussion was brief. Apparently, they had not gathered to share feelings of guilt. They broke apart again to enter the strange animals.

He cursed himself for not ridding the forest of the initial invaders when he'd had the chance—perhaps this would have stalled the advent of these brutes who'd killed his trees so viciously. But how was he to know that men existed who could control such giant beasts?

This war was unlike any his father had ever warned him about. And he was unsure how to stop these men.

Upon this hopeless realization, despair overrode his passion to avenge. One could not fight a war when his heart and soul were riddled with grief. His body felt as if it had been chopped apart just like the trees. Just like in his dream.

Adding to the confusion was the rumbling sound that had erupted from the vicinity of his enemies—not thunder nor a shake from the planet's core—but a loud, steady roar that hurt his ears.

And before he could guess what caused it, the men and their great beasts rumbled away, obscured by the clouds of dust and debris caused by their passing. They took the bodies of his trees and left him with an emptiness devoid of life and full of regret.

He should have been ready. He could have prevented this.

The desolation they'd left was far more disturbing than the silence of his deserted village, at least for that he'd been prepared.

This was much different, like someone had cut a chunk from his body when he hadn't been paying attention, without considering that the chunk was needed to sustain the whole. It was an emptiness so devastating that he knew the effects of it would spread—both inside himself and all around him.

He had missed the chance to prevent their onslaught. He had allowed their entrance into his forest, tricked by their pitiful demeanors, and they had taken advantage of his oversight and killed hundreds of his trees.

The wasteland before him was barren of life and littered with wounds.

CHAPTER TWENTY-ONE

EVERY SO OFTEN when prompted by her heart, Raela left words of encouragement on the wall for Rebial to find. Sometimes she did this just to satisfy her longing, sometimes it was to express the bitterness that came with missing him.

But on one particularly bleak day she dropped a small bead and paused to write, not out of wistfulness, but to relieve herself of stress.

> *The babies are missing. Four of them—snatched by the planet. We search but there is not a trace, not even a foul smell that would implicate a tribesman. You know which one I mean.*

The words portrayed a strange and disturbing scenario— one so terrible that it had to be happening to someone else. Except that it wasn't, and the burden seemed insurmountable at times. Releasing the words on stone repaired some of the emptiness inside her. She hoped their meaning wouldn't deter him. How long had they even been gone?

Inside a cave, the concept of time fades like a memory. No longer does the sun or moon suggest when one should have a meal or try to sleep. For several days, the tribe's internal clock seemed to have them functioning on a schedule, but after a while, the steady gloom of dark tunnels only perpetuated a mind-numbing eternity.

Their habits grew sporadic and undisciplined as a result.

Raela discovered that time is a scary thing when you have too much of it. Especially when the spaces you fill seem never ending. She continued to direct the tribe through dark passages, but the repetition of their surroundings only worsened their sense of monotony.

At times the route felt circuitous, and based on her memory of the map, it was. They crawled through narrow tunnels and rounded corners that seemed unnecessary ventures, prolonged their destination for days. But it was her duty to lead them as the prophecy had intended. And it directed them into nooks and crannies that reminded them of places in their minds they'd attempted to forget.

For what wasn't largely discussed was a part of the prophecy that many tribal members refused to acknowledge. It had been carefully overlooked for many years, purposely avoided. The trade-in, as you would call it, or the payment for such. For nature does not give without sacrifice. And the truth was a bitter, painful thing. And it was much easier to forget or set aside this knowledge than endure the tribulations of this forbidden obligation.

No one was sure how to fulfill this obligation. No one wanted to consider it either. Although the women made every attempt to thwart the inevitability of conception once they learned it was time to obey the prophecy, stomachs continued to grow large and round, with protective arms bound tightly around them.

Some gave birth just before their descent into the cave.

These poor mothers could not revel in the happiness but instead were forced to wallow in fear. Some were almost ready to birth their children as they walked the tunnels, and these women Raela sympathized with the most.

It was far too painful to think about, and since the specifics had not been elaborated on, neither in the prophecy nor within her grandfather's vision, there was really nothing more to do than wait and hope it would be forgotten. Perhaps the old seer had misread the signs. Perhaps what he had relayed to them merely symbolized something they could not fully understand. It was possible even that the obligation was more in spirit. It was best not to second guess nature, best not to question.

And so they'd lived their lives peacefully above ground, but not without acknowledging there was a dangerous cloud hovering in the air above them, one that was presently calm but would eventually burst, sending streams of agony down until it soaked their clothes and skin and all there was left to do was cry.

What was unclear happened soon enough. For every time they faced necessity and found themselves in a tunnel that seemed to stray from their more direct route, one of the babies wound up missing. Nature only took the very young, the tiny bundles that had been born nearest the time they had begun their descent. Somehow these children fell through the cracks, were discreetly snatched away despite tight arms that held them close. Not even a parting whimper or a lock of hair remained.

Of course, Vandor had been interrogated since he was the only one among them who may have had an interest in untimely deaths. He had adamantly denied any wrongdoings, had even offered himself up to supervision. So the men from the tribe took turns watching him, making sure he was truly innocent. And, surprisingly, he was.

Despite the sadness that prevailed among the tribe, Raela found a semblance of peace during these times, for Vandor could not watch her when he was being monitored.

Still, the babies came up missing during the strangest of times.

When the tribe was dying of thirst, they came upon a pool of clear water so pure it reflected its surroundings with majestic clarity. They gathered around and took turns wetting their tongues, filling their empty casks, pouring the water down their dry and scratchy throats. After they'd quenched their thirst and said thanks to this enormous bit of luck, it came to light that someone—a very tiny female— was missing from her mother's arms. Loud wails of distress erupted and reverberated through the passage until all there was left to do was persevere.

When the air became stuffy and the coughing started, their lungs about ready to burst, they came upon an area in which the air began circulating once again, as if the cave itself had formed natural vents. So grateful they were to breathe freely that a tribal member felt compelled to tell a story about the fresh air above ground. As they reminisced, a father bounced his boy into the air to keep the child from crying out. The boy disappeared during the telling of the tale. His once doting parents could not be consoled. Only continuing onward healed the bitter wounds growing in their hearts.

As hunger ravaged them, causing them to think unhealthy thoughts, they came upon a cavern most peculiar. Plants grew from cracks in tunnels, seemingly sprouting from nothing or dust grazing on stone. Once the tribe had plucked and distributed the fruits, they barely had time to finish swallowing their scant meal before noticing another boy was no longer in his mother's woven cradle. Her cries produced enough tears to water a small forest had they the means to grow one.

The final taking of a child from the tribe happened a great deal of time later. Their torches burning low, it seemed the darkness would soon overwhelm and conquer their spirits. As the last torch died out, the tribe collapsed in agony upon stone. The blackness surrounding them was too much. The motivation to continue had died with the fire. But then someone's hand slid across the bumpy ground and found a healthy stash of wood suitable for igniting flames.

The light uplifted them, gave them a reason to proceed. They picked themselves back up, along with as many bundles of wood that they could carry, and continued walking. Barely several paces in, a new mother looked down to where she had so tightly clutched her baby girl and saw that she was gone. Her cries of distress rang to deafening proportions, but they were the last to be heard for some time.

After that, the tribe focused intently on advancing through the tunnels. After bearing these losses, there was nothing left to do but move past the trauma and leave it behind them. It did not occur to them that their deprivation of life's necessities had vanished along with the babies, though Raela dared to consider it inside her own thoughts. It would be rude to voice it, that someone else's pain was for the betterment of the whole.

So she kept her mouth shut, finding comfort in patting her own stomach. It helped her cope with all the pain and brought her peace of mind.

So as the tribe continued, no longer did they hunger, no longer did they thirst. Their breaths stayed even, and their torches burned strong.

CHAPTER TWENTY-TWO

REBIAL STAGGERED BACK toward the village. The woods were silent around him, as if they knew he'd let them down. Not even an ancestor gave him the ghost of a pat on the back. He'd not had contact with any member of his tribe for weeks now. To say he needed encouragement from someone was an understatement.

He supposed he could end his suffering and seek out his tribe. Still, he refused to look inside the tree where Raela had stashed the prophecy. His stubbornness was the only thing that would not abandon him.

How could he join the others after witnessing the atrocity that had occurred in his homeland? The beautiful trees he had admired, in awe of their stature, had been ripped from the ground quicker than he could avenge their deaths. This was destroying the soil. This was destroying his soul. The invaders had come when he was sleeping—huge numbers of them with their massive, yellow beasts—and demolished part of what he loved.

His heart cried out for Raela. He murmured her name and felt the grass poke his feet in response. Perhaps it was her pain echoing back at him through the dirt.

But it was not just her that he missed. Even a familiar face would satisfy his loneliness.

Feeling defeated, he stopped at a babbling stream. If he had the energy, he'd wade through it, but instead he perched on a large rock jutting out from a mingling of dirt and sand. He buried his head in his hands. His body fell limp. Perhaps the time had come for him to accept defeat, admit he was in over his head.

The war I'm fighting is too big for me to combat by myself.

The thought depleted him further. Sorrow carved the features of his face. An unfamiliar wetness spurted from the corners of his eyes. He had not cried since his father's death. It enraged him these tears were betraying the pact he'd made with his soul.

Something brushed against him. Its length dragged along his back and curled lightly around him in a way that caused shivers to creep up his spine. There was a shifting of sand. A quiver of air fluttered past.

Lifting his face from his palms, he found himself staring into the wide and tawny face of a cougar. Hair stood on the back of his neck. He sat deathly still, waiting to see if it would attack.

The cat stared evenly back. Its presence radiated an intensity he had once felt within himself.

He maneuvered into a position that would enable him to spring if need be, crouched atop the rock, all the while keeping his eyes locked with the cat. The yellow flecks around its pupils expelled deep wisdom.

As an adult, he had never been so close to one of the animals. The times in his youth, he did not fully remember. The memory of him playing with a few cubs while the mother cleaned herself nearby lay within a vast fog inside his mind. He had not disputed the validity of this memory since others had confirmed it. In later years, he'd engaged in harmless pursuits with the animals—a sort of hide and seek game that never had a winner or a loser.

Despite all this, and perhaps because of his recent failure, he felt afraid. It occurred to him that some of the animal's prey in the forest had probably ventured away once the killers had begun their attack. The cat was probably hungry. Perhaps the game would soon be over. It was time for him to lose and this powerful animal to win. He nodded slowly in agreement with his concession. He may as well allow the cat another meal since he was unsure of his own will to live.

"Go ahead, devour me," he said impassively.

He sank back to a seated position, averted his gaze. Then he waited for sharp teeth to go for the vein running through his neck. Paws would soon tear at his flesh. What he readied himself for did not occur. Time moved just as slowly as before. He lifted his head, bewildered.

Three cats now sat on their haunches before him. Like perfect statues, they stared at him expectantly. They had safety in numbers—if cats concerned themselves with such things—yet still did not attack. Their casual demeanor squashed his distress.

He placed his feet firmly on the ground and stood. Power flowed back into his limbs, shot up through his feet and dispersed throughout his entire being. The cougars stood then too.

He understood now what was happening. These cats also understood, not only who he was as a person and why he remained, but what was happening to their forest. They had come to his aid. They would follow him, attack with him, kill with him. And he would gladly accept their help.

He allowed them to escort him back to the village, gave them several slabs of fresh meat from a recent hunt. Then he sat beside a crackling fire and plotted how to kill their next invader.

❧

> *Our flesh and bone have dissolved. So it seems. We walk as ghosts who need not. All my desires have waned but for one. That is you. How long before you seek out your tribesmen? How could you allow me to leave you behind? What do you have to live for now besides hate and death? Funny you choose death. Life grows in my belly while hate thrives in your heart. But perhaps you have learned to respect the prophecy and are on your way.*

This was not the way Raela would have liked to break the news to Rebial, that she was carrying his child, but it felt satisfying to reveal the truth.

Of course, she had done so when no one was watching, when the rest of the tribe, even Vandor, had pushed ahead.

Her mother had long given up trying to persuade her to stop lagging so far behind the others. The embarrassment of her daughter's wounded spirit had compelled the woman to distance herself. Or perhaps she felt guilt over waiting to tell the truth about the grandfather's death.

Raela stopped overthinking her mother's motivations, for she preferred the solitude. It was better than having someone judgmental walking alongside you.

Sometimes she wondered if her mother resented being skipped as the chosen scribe. Perhaps she thought she could do better—if only she'd been the one born with the mark. Raela dared not dwell on what could have been.

The knocking in her belly had come when she was walking by herself, daydreaming of her past life with Rebial, trying to ignore the despair that hung like a dark cloud over everything.

It came as if to remind her that Rebial was not the only one worthy of her attention.

At first, she thought perhaps she was hungry, but not even a gurgle came forth to validate that assumption.

With wide eyes, she remembered that her cycle had never come. It was many days past due, weeks even, as the prophecy and their travels had consumed her mind. Perhaps she had subconsciously attributed her monthly absence to there being many things she once desired that her body no longer craved.

Her stomach stirred again, and she instinctively placed her palm against her belly. One gentle nudge pushed back, and the knowledge she was responsible for more than just herself now came over her. Heat grazed her forehead though the air was cool. She kept walking, thoughts now swirling so fast they almost made her dizzy.

It would be difficult carrying his child, difficult keeping this secret from the others. She would hide her condition as long as her physical bearing allowed. It was only one more thing to hide after all.

She felt like she would burst from keeping secrets. There were secrets in her mind. A secret now in her belly. Of course, there was no need to conceal the secret in her heart.

For even though the tribe should be happy for her— their scribe who'd left behind her love for them and traveled alone without her grandfather—she knew they would not look upon her kindly. There would be no fondness for her nor the child once they knew the truth.

A bitterness had invaded them after spending so much time beneath the ground. They were used to being sur-rounded by lush, green vegetation, not cramped together in such confined spaces. And the pain that had come with losing the babies had only deepened the bitterness.

Perhaps if her grandfather had been there, he could have consoled them, reminded them the reason they suffered was for the benefit of everyone. He'd voice what she was too ashamed to say aloud. What had happened would benefit the children who had not been stolen. The debt they'd paid would even benefit her own.

But her grandfather was not with them. The pain she felt from his loss had still not healed. And Raela did not have the same visionary mind he did. She was not as respected. If the tribe knew the truth, that she had left behind the book, they would feel the opposite of consoled.

And so this gentle knocking terrified her, despite the hope that came with it, for it would only add to the outrage they would inflict upon her when they found out.

Unless, of course, her lover came and rescued her from the shame and repercussions she was bound to suffer from the choices that she'd made.

CHAPTER TWENTY-THREE

TO BLEND IN easier with his surroundings, Rebial took to the practice of rubbing moss thickly on his skin. He coated his arms and legs, even spread it across his face. The moss served its purpose well, hid him effectively from his enemies.

It was his form of warpaint since the tribal elders had deprived him of having the right to wear it based on tradition. Instead of a bold and dangerous red streaked across his cheeks, his color would be forest green and it would be all-encompassing. To trick his opponents, he would use the forest in every way he could.

His enemies—who now launched attacks on individual trees after that first devastating assault—never noticed Rebial until the havoc he created was underway. By then, it was too late for them to do anything about it.

These men came on foot all by themselves or in smaller numbers. Though he assumed they must be lesser beings— for large beasts did not accompany them—this did not deter him from launching an attack. If they resisted and scattered like ants in all directions, the big cats found them.

He had stopped feeling guilty about sabotaging his enemies when they were unsuspecting. He'd taken on the big cats' strategy and realized that fighting as nature meant that compassion no longer mattered. He fought only to achieve an end result. The end justifying the means is nature's cruel reality. It sustains or kills as if both were the same.

The moss was sticky, enabling him to climb trees with little effort once his hands were covered. He had always climbed trees, but now he did so as a hunter—quick and agile—having learned this skill from the big cats through his constant interaction with them. He jumped higher than ever before, attributing this newly acquired feat to what he'd learned from the animals.

That wasn't all; the cats now helped him with the hunt. Skulking in the treetops, he became adept at scoping out the whereabouts of his enemies long before even they had decided where they planned to go.

The cougars' instincts became his, and he wondered whether he was now part cat. They slept outside his hut at night, nudging him awake when the enemy came earlier than he was accustomed to rising in the morning.

Almost every evening, Rebial washed the forest from his skin before he slept. Even though he had no one to impress, no one to associate with in a way that did not involve war, he still felt the desire to be clean. It reminded him he was human, though this remembrance also came with the familiar emotions that a human has—fear, guilt, remorse—feelings he had no use for when he was constantly avenging.

After a particularly brutal fight—in which he and his cats each earned a kill—he'd done an unusual thing and neglected washing due to heavy fatigue. Thus, with no one to scold him, he'd gone to bed unclean.

At the riverside the next morning, he stripped down

before entering the cool water. He scrubbed his arms, but the moss clung onto him tighter than ever before. He rubbed vigorously but to no avail.

His own puzzled expression reflected back at him amid the ripples. He waded until the water rose higher and washed over his entire body. Perhaps after a good soak, he could wipe himself clean.

After several minutes, he scrubbed an arm again, but the moss held strong. It was embedded in his flesh so deeply that it seemed futile to continue scrubbing. Flustered, he looked down at his green body, but the longer he stared, the more he flowed and swayed, until his image as a man dispersed into bubbles.

Alarmed, he burst from the water, a man again, but with skin that truly matched the greenery of the woods.

Except his feet were mounds of sands. Lifting one upward, it turned back into a foot.

His panic mixed with confusion. He began to run. Faster and faster until the scenery blurred around him. So fast he realized he was no longer a man running, but a gathering of leaves blowing with the breeze. His inhalations overwhelmed him, caused him to puff up larger and larger until he was so exhilarated that the leaves disbanded, and he tripped.

He found himself on the forest floor, arms sprawled as roots wedged in the soil. He snapped them loose and sprang to his feet.

Terror gripped him. He spun and panted, afraid to stand still. His surroundings heaved in proportion to his frantic gasps and racing thoughts.

What is happening to me?

Staggering to a tree, he placed his hand upon its trunk

to steady himself. His limb stiffened as bark spread across it. Lurching backward, he ripped it free with a crack. His toes branched into the ground like roots. He wrenched them away and stumbled.

He belted out an agonized howl that reverberated and echoed.

The sky darkened. Treetops shuddered overhead. Branches bent crookedly. Leaves picked up and swirled about. Insects buzzed his eardrums in proportion to his breath. He tasted dry wood. Ripped and clawed through vegetation. The harder he resisted, the more intensely the forest gripped him. Until exhausted, he closed his eyes and sank into the dirt.

I must be imagining this. I must be dreaming.

As he stilled his mind, the soil quivered all around him. Worms wriggled as if squirming in and out of his flesh. His thoughts coursed through dirt and mycelium until it reached a prophecy in roots. It pumped life into him like the steady beating of a heart.

Raela had placed it there for him. The thought calmed him.

He opened his eyes, breathed a sigh of acceptance and saw himself for what he truly was. His hair and skin resembled patterns of bark and leaves. If he looked at his arm or foot for any length of time, it blended in with the surroundings. He was slowly becoming a part of it, mingling with nature itself.

But with calmer thoughts, his image stabilized as a man.

The only way he could remain himself was to embrace what was happening to him. And so he would. It was then he accepted he was no longer separate from the forest. Like the big cats, it had befriended him in a way in which there was no turning back. They had joined.

This also meant he was part of the prophecy too, despite his distaste for it. They were, the three of them, altogether one.

He stood. His cougars were nearby. They circled round and sniffed him. Purred with satisfaction at who he had become.

Every unwanted entrance into his woods thereafter was like a bug crawling on him, nosing around, looking for something to take and exploit. Every cut into a tree was like a gash into his skin.

He felt it all and vowed to avenge every broken blade of grass now, every plant torn from his soil.

Death was no longer a last resort. It was a way to handle these transgressions. Mercy was not something nature practiced, and so neither would Rebial.

Whenever his enemies harmed or destroyed part of the forest, he felt the pain stronger than just in his heart. It was now his pain as well. And it increased every day still, stronger and stronger until his rage could be felt by the invaders. They did not like the feeling this strange forest gave them. Yet they proceeded with their killings just as brashly as before, chopping trees with careless ease until he appeared before them.

Sometimes they kept chopping, after a slight head shake or rubbing of their eyes, in denial of the man who was part forest. But their failure to acknowledge his warped existence only increased Rebial's fury. For his sacrifice to lose himself inside his passion should not be so easily ignored.

Only when they truly saw him did he feel vindicated, when their horror mixed with fascination mirrored his twisted plight as a man melded with woods.

❧

Rubbing her belly absently, Raela paused when she came upon the midwife standing at the bend of a tunnel one day holding a torch. The woman's gaze was sharp and clear upon her, scanning her up and down as if she had every right to do so.

She said a silent sorry to her child for putting its existence in jeopardy and sucked her pregnant belly in.

The midwife said nothing as she approached, compelling Raela to believe that she had fooled her. She smiled to herself, glad her secret could maintain some semblance of longevity.

Then her appreciation came crashing down.

"They will crucify you for it," the midwife said.

Raela felt that silent fear course through her. Which secret had the midwife discovered? Panic joined her fear, but then the midwife glanced down at Raela's belly as if to clarify the statement. Suddenly she knew what Rebial must have felt, the strong bond of protection that can be so overwhelming. She felt this for her unborn child.

"I did nothing wrong," she whispered.

"Jealousy does not always sprout from wrongdoing. It merely happens when someone does not like what you have."

"I have nothing," she quickly said.

"Not yet," the midwife said, "but you will soon. I can tell."

"I won't tell them," Raela responded, glad that at least one secret stayed safe for now. "And you best not either."

"I will not have to. Unlike other kinds of secrets, one like this can only be kept for so long."

Raela gazed solemnly at the midwife then, wondering if this was a hint that the woman did know more. She strained her brain, trying to recollect whether anyone had seen her leave the prophecy in the tree. Of course, they hadn't, or someone would have snatched it back up, already accused her of having committed such a selfish deed. No one would go willingly into the depths of the planet just so they could die there.

She decided to try and gain the midwife's sympathy. After all, she could no longer count on receiving it from her own mother.

"Will you help me?"

The midwife twisted her mouth in distaste. "You should have refrained. Or used an herb to protect yourself. Who will father the child?"

Raela scanned her surroundings desperately, aggravated at the midwife for throwing this in her face. She wanted to prove she'd thought ahead, defend Rebial, mention he still had a chance to redeem himself to the tribe.

"The child will be taken care of," she said with confidence.

As her temper softened, she let out a breath, knowing she'd reacted correctly and kept her composure.

"I cannot help you, but I will not sabotage you either," the midwife finally said.

At the moment, this was all Raela could ask of her.

"I appreciate that," she replied. "Just know that I think he will follow us. So the child won't be without a father forever."

But instead of challenging this assertion, the midwife asked, "How will he know the way?"

Raela just looked at the midwife blankly, for there was

nothing convincing she could say without revealing her other secret.

"He'll just know it," she said simply.

The midwife lowered her gaze as if Raela were delusional, which she much preferred to the woman knowing the truth. The look still stung and made her feel ashamed.

"Thank you for keeping my secret," she said.

The midwife responded with a swift nod that implied their talk was over. She turned to venture deeper into the tunnel.

But as Raela followed gingerly behind, she noticed Vandor lurking not so far ahead. The midwife walked past him as if he were invisible, and Raela wondered if he had heard.

The sly smirk on his face suggested that he had, yet it wasn't unusual for Vandor's face to hold that expression. How was it she yearned so strongly for a man so quick to desert her yet was forced to endure the unwanted attentions of another? Why was her luck so cruel?

Not only was his interest unending, but she was certain Vandor did not pay attention for positive reasons.

Raela patted her belly reflexively when she felt her child kick, for it was sudden and more urgent than the times before.

Vandor was watching too. Of course, he was. Raela sucked in her gut, annoyed she had not a moment to enjoy by herself with her unborn child.

His gaze rested on her belly then, his expression puzzled, which she took to mean he had not heard her conversation with the midwife after all.

She tossed her shoulder between them as she scraped past him in the narrow tunnel. For not much longer would she be able to hide the truth, especially now, if this offensive man would not leave her alone.

CHAPTER TWENTY-FOUR

THE MAN HOLDING the long-toothed blade caught something out of the corner of his eye run past. It was near his size yet darted with the swiftness of a bug. He lowered his saw.

He had been preparing to slice into the side of a tree, opposite of where he and Tom had cut the wedge that would direct the fall away from where they stood.

Of course, at present, Tom was standing somewhere else. Nature had called.

"I'll be right back, Dan," he'd said before disappearing into the trees. "Got to take a leak."

But Dan didn't want to think about why Tom hadn't returned yet. Instead, he turned his attention back to the tree.

Normally trees this old weren't allowed to be hacked down. But times had changed. Standards had dropped. No one cared about trees anymore or ecosystems, for that matter. People who no longer even liked themselves could not be expected to revere nature.

He certainly no longer gave a shit. Loving nature was

delusional— a childish fantasy the harsh world managed to pulverize over time into sheepish ideals.

The distraction must have been a deer. Tom had never moved that fast in his life. Hence why he hadn't yet returned. On another day in another forest, a deer might be his focus. But today, he was after wood.

He positioned his saw on the bulky trunk that rivaled the size of a house. He and Tom had chosen to saw through it like their forefathers, the old way, like real men. They'd snap a picture. Go back to power tools tomorrow.

The fleeting image came again, breaking his concentration. He paused to consider his next move.

His boss had said there was nothing to fear. All the predatory animals had migrated away once the workers had begun their steady progression, and the primitive people who were believed to be living deep inside the forest had not been found. It was almost as if the forest had swallowed them up. Men had roamed for days on end, searching for them—well, maybe for a few days anyway—not that it would have mattered had they been found.

The government had been intent on exploiting old-growth forests to keep up with the growing demand for wood. Some big wig had laid out the cash, which meant it was time to lay down the forest. The tribal people not existing anymore—apparently just a naive fantasy after all—had just sped up the process, left out all the deceitful negotiating outlined in paperwork they wouldn't be able to read anyway.

Having distracted himself from the previous disturbance, he heaved his saw up and finally wedged it into the trunk. He jiggled the blade until it cut further through the bark. The work was strenuous. His muscles tensed as he strained to move the saw towards the center. He barely moved it an inch.

Where the hell was Tom?

Something brushed past his thigh. He jumped and almost let go of the saw. Then he quickly scanned the area around him. Although there was nothing out of the ordinary in sight, the overwhelming quietude surrounding him was not comforting. Sweat beaded rapidly upon his forehead.

"It's from all the hard work," he muttered.

Turning back to the tree, he began splitting its flesh once more. Another inch. Tom had better hurry up, or he'd be taking the picture. Above the groan of his saw, he heard branches snap behind him. Then pounding like someone was running toward him.

He whipped around uneasily, left his saw jutting halfway from the trunk, and proceeded to pull a much smaller blade out of a leather holster attached to his outer thigh.

He was not in the mood for this. He was here for the glory and couldn't afford to be distracted by rogue animals or fellow lumberjacks playing games.

Something ran across his line of vision once more. This time the image was less obstructed. That being the case, it was still hard for him to grasp exactly what it was because it blended so easily into the scenery.

He followed slowly, sweat now dripping from his face, his hand clenching the knife. He was sure it was just a trick, either by his so-called friend Tom or by the environment itself, since being in this type of seclusion for extended periods could have an impact on one's senses.

He stepped around a tree. This time he caught a better view. What appeared to be the outline of a man moved carefully away from him.

"Nice camouflage outfit," he said with a smirk.

Now that he knew it was just someone playing a joke on him, his worry subsided. He hoped whoever it was would reveal themselves before they forced him to use his weapon. If the perpetrator happened to be for real, well, there were plenty of places to stash the body.

Tom may be slow, but he had never been a snitch.

The camouflaged man appeared again, just yards away, with what could only be described as a nefarious smile. Dan reflexively backed up, realizing he'd never even used that word before.

The disturbing smile grew even larger as the man slunk closer, the scenery rippling around him. His appearance changed just as rapidly as his immediate background. Alternating shades of brown and green. Both his skin and clothes textured like bark and leaves.

"Shit," Dan said, backing up again.

This was no camouflaged man but a thing from childhood stories—a green man of the woods.

Confusion gripped his awareness, kept him from attacking. Or perhaps fear froze him in place.

The green man lunged towards him suddenly. His flight instinct took over. *To hell with Tom.* With a burst of speed, he turned to run. Not taking the time to get a clear sense of direction, he ran like he had seen a ghost. Or something worse.

He knew this thing was something worse.

Glancing over his shoulder, he continued running wildly. The thing was gaining on him. Reached toward him with whittled fingers.

Something spliced into his stomach. His forehead banged against a trunk. Choked sounds gurgled from his throat as he struggled to breathe. Miraculously, he remained upright. Perhaps he'd make it after all. But then the hazy realization of being stuck to his own saw's jagged teeth washed over him. Blood gushed from his wound and sprayed the trunk.

He tried to wriggle free but only succeeded in shredding his innards. His surroundings blurred. One final thought consumed him. That thing, whatever it was—a forest man or spirit of the woods—had played him like a fool. Led him in a circle. Controlled him like a puppet. Disoriented him on purpose. Caused him to gouge himself as mercilessly as he'd gouged the tree.

Perhaps that had been the point.

He looked around as best he could to gain some understanding of what had killed him. But all he saw as his last breath faded was his blood dripping and seeping into the soil. Then his world spun, and he was gone.

The woman who hovered at the side of the tunnel, waiting for Raela to near, had once been a young mother. Now she was a broken shell of her former self. Deep lines burdened her features, and her smile was frail as if the corners of her mouth held it in place with great effort.

Raela had to respect that effort, for she had been struggling with her own mood lately.

"What can I do for you, Nola?" she asked gently so as to not adversely impact the woman's quivering lips.

She couldn't do much to help the woman, but she was willing to do all that she could.

"May I see it?" Nola asked, nodding gently in her direction while lowering her gaze. "Will you get it out and show me?"

Raela froze in horror as the woman looked ravenously at her midsection. She placed her hand on her stomach and took a step back.

"You must be unwell," she responded.

Nola moved closer, eyes focused and unblinking, her expression crazed. She reached a hand outward as if she wanted to rip Raela's child from its womb.

"I'm not unwell," Nola replied. "I just want to see what belongs to me."

Her pleasant tone made Raela want to vomit, but she swallowed it back down.

"It doesn't belong to you," she said.

Was this woman so sick in the mind now, that she truly thought Raela carried her own baby? Had the midwife cruelly told her? Would she claim that all the babies were hers? Where were the others?

As Nola stepped closer, Raela's heart thudded in her chest.

"It is mine," Nola insisted. "It belongs to all of us."

Raela clutched her stomach tighter. "You're wrong," she whispered.

"Why are you being so mean to me?" Nola asked, looking flustered.

Raela shook her head and bit her lip.

Only inches away now, Nola lurched forward to poke impatiently at Raela's beaded bag. "Let me see the passage in the prophecy. The one about the stolen babies."

Raela's breath caught, and she struggled to release it. At least the woman wasn't trying to take her unborn child, but even though Nola's demand was not so terrible, she still had nothing to offer. Without meaning to, she glanced down at the woman's sunken belly—empty of child, but still bearing the extra weight of having so recently borne one.

Nola acknowledged Raela's mistake. Her eyes registered hurt and pain. She crossed her arms over her belly as if to shield it from Raela's prying gaze.

"Well," she said unkindly now, "is it not obvious why I might find comfort in its words?"

Raela nodded dumbly. "Of course, it is."

"Where is it then?" Nola asked.

"Nola, I'm so sorry," Raela said, "but I can't show it to you."

Nola's eyes flashed angry daggers. "Why? I thought only you were to carry it. Who has it then?"

"I can't say," Raela said truthfully. She hoped Rebial, but it may be too soon to cater to such wishes.

Nola seemed unable to contain herself, looked this way and that, gripped her hands open and closed. Raela waited to be battered by an onslaught of words.

But none came.

Instead, Nola bowed her head when the tears came, whimpered softly, and stumbled away.

Raela bore the weight of the other women's nasty glares throughout the rest of the day. Her mother's presence grew even more distant now, perhaps consumed by the other women's bad perception of her. It was clear they judged her action as a way of being spiteful.

The whispers came, insensitive and cruel.

She left her heart back with her lover.

Why would she deprive poor Nola of something that might repair her despair?

But Raela could not defend herself. Pregnancy, and the emotional ride that came with it, had blinded her to

Nola's true intentions. She was troubled by the vulgarity of her misinterpretation. And defending herself by revealing she had left the prophecy behind would only put her in a difficult position. They would hate her for it. And with emotions so high, she dared not provoke them any further.

It was best to remain silent and pretend she did not see their accusing looks, especially the one the midwife was giving her which was mixed with both disgust and bewilderment. It was best to ignore Nola's sniveling that traveled back to her in weak, distressing fragments.

She would maintain her secret for as long as she could.

CHAPTER TWENTY-FIVE

IT HAD BEEN weeks. Time flew by quicker than Rebial was able to keep track. Night and day melted together. Raela had vanished out of his sight but had not deleted herself from his mind.

He saw her walking through dimly lit passageways in his dreams, lugging bags and grasping onto the hands of others. He saw her curled up on dusty stone, sleeping blissfully, her hair pulled back and knotted as she slept, her hands clenched into tiny balls pressed against the bottom of her chin. Sometimes he saw her crying. Tears would stream down her face, and he would feel a pull to join her.

When he said her name out loud, she cringed. Even if he said it so softly that he, himself, could barely hear it, her shoulders bunched together, and her elbows dug into her sides.

She came to his mind in the darkness, sometimes even when he was waiting for the intruders. But with the onset of the enemy, things changed. It wasn't long before he thought of her less and less. He was busy protecting, busy avenging, busy hating. For a time, his hate weighed heavier than his love.

This only managed to speed up his transformation.

His fingers were now spindly twigs. His hair straggled like wisps of vegetation. His skin was thickly grooved not with the wrinkles of an old man, but the strength and solidity of a giant tree. His flesh now changed between different shades of brown and green. He melted in and out of sight, camouflaged, as the forest accepted him in and out of its bounty, as if it were one entity of vegetation.

He could emerge from the bark of one tree and escape into another. When he spoke, his voice rasped like wood creaking and leaves rustling. Words only came out with great force.

Insects buzzed by his ears, told him short bursts of phrases that he now understood.

They're coming.

These humans that invaded his woods did not have the rich, melodic voice of certain members of his tribe. Their voices, their characters even, were as thin as slivers of wood, as unsubstantial as a flake of stone. Though they had eyes, they did not see the forest for what it truly was.

It was more than just a supply of lumber to make boats or dwellings or however they intended to use the bodies of trees. Its ability to provide for material things was only a small fraction of what it had to offer. But this type of human did not possess the sight needed to know such things—they were blind fools chopping and killing with no care to the repercussions of their actions.

The trees fell in the most unpredictable manner when their trunks were sliced through. The directions in which they toppled defied gravity, but they did fall within the liking of Rebial. Every time one crashed down onto his enemy, it reminded him of his own foot crunching down on swarms of ants. If a tree must fall, he had decided long ago, he would determine where.

Cries of pain and suffering went unheard over the methods used to cause them.

Watch out!

Help!

What is that thing?

It was all garble to Rebial. By the time a tree stopped creaking and crashed onto the forest floor, the human who had uttered these words was dead. Trees the width of many bodies wiped out hordes of invaders when they landed. But if he could prevent a tree from falling, he would do so by exposing himself to them.

Even his own people had felled a tree to make a hut or canoe from time to time. Still, there were trees so old they were considered ancestors, trees you did not touch.

These men did not choose wisely.

It still took time for the invaders to see him when he walked within their midst. Blending in as well as he did, he was at first invisible. But he couldn't move around them forever without being noticed eventually. Even the senses of humans as clueless as these would notice a flicker of movement that didn't quite match the surroundings.

Once he caught their eye, they at least knew something peculiar was happening. And before, when he would try so desperately for them to see him, he would prove with savage violence that he was more than an illusion.

But he had long ago stopped trying to emerge so forcefully. It was more effective to trick them, watching them twitch and squirm, poking at their perception as he became more apparent until he was finally noticed in full form. This was when he did not bother hiding any longer.

He wove in and out of vegetation, confusing what was happening even more. For who could touch this strange green man who took the shape of a tree one moment, the rigid structure of a jagged cliff the next?

They'd point and shout, drop their sharp blades and either run toward him or away. Their most dangerous weapon was their jagged saw, but in the heat of battle, they didn't have the wherewithal to use it.

His ability to confuse them provoked a greater sense of uneasiness and impacted their ability to retaliate. And once he had jarred them so, and they could see their efforts to combat him were ineffective, their uneasiness was replaced with fear.

No matter which direction they fled, Rebial always found a way to catch them, for he could weave in and out of the forest with the grace of a deer, the stealth of a big cat. These cougars, his friends, preferred to maintain their habits of taking a swift bite from behind—a bite meant to kill, not to tease. Rebial preferred to do the latter first. It was more satisfying that way.

For what was the point of killing without first seeing acknowledgment paint across his victim's faces? The recognition they had erred and stepped foot inside his forest without his permission? Not only his but his tribe's, should they so choose to come back. They had invaded not only his homeland but the whole of nature itself, the entity that had underestimated his prowess and capabilities. Yet he was certain nature relished in his successes with him as he defended it with glory.

Perhaps if the rest of the tribe had been at his skill level—his fellow warriors who had so easily bowed out— then they could have prevented the attacks so thoroughly that the others could have remained and lived in peace. Although Rebial was doing quite a fine job all by himself. Yet this truth baffled him more and more every day. For why was it then that he was doing this alone?

When his enemies ran from him, he followed. Appearing here, then there, before their eyes in ways they knew were purely unnatural. He would lock eyes, see fear cascade over their faces, then allow a tree branch to slice down slowly. He needed them to recognize what was happening, perhaps even see a glint of irony—they had come into his forest as predators and died as prey.

Although most did not consider a forest worth thinking about when their life flashed before their eyes. He knew this because the closer they became to being one with the forest, not like him but in death, he could see their memories flash within his own mind.

They were odd visions, foreign to him, alien-like, portraying strange places and adornments. Yet these visions and spectacles—with their flashing colors and shiny, whirring objects—lacked the life-giving force that resided inside a forest.

And it was clear that most did not have the intelligence to self-reflect on such a matter. Those who owned too much did not consider their own trespass. They had the mindset of a pest, a bug, a flea.

And so, during their final moments, he was devoted to exposing the fallacy of their ways.

You have set foot where you don't belong, he'd tell them. You have soiled my forest with your presence, he'd say. You have sought to kill the memories of my ancestors. You have invaded my homeland with your jagged tools and giant beasts. You've stomped on what was precious to us, what sustained life by growing helpful plants that hid in thoughtful places.

You have infected the forest with your presence, like a small tick upon its body, sucking the life force from something great, so crucial to life and longevity and all the plants and animals you see around you.

And some invaders did hear these strange crackling wisps of sound as blood leaked from their wounds to soak the dirt. Rebial might catch a final sputter of recognition before their eyes finally closed to meet the black death they so deserved.

In a forest, death provides life. Yet Rebial's burgeoning forest was now focused entirely on death.

CHAPTER TWENTY-SIX

"WHY WON'T YOU allow a grieving mother one moment of comfort?" the elder asked, the torch he held illuminating his stern expression. "Have you no sense of decency?"

Raela looked away, unable to hold his gaze.

He had pulled her into an adjacent cavern to privately ask the dreaded question. It was one she'd known would come eventually, but she was still surprised at how difficult it was to answer. Yet she also was surprised by her lack of shame.

"If I refused to let her see it," she said, "it's because I have good reason."

"There is no good reason," the elder snapped. "You do not own it. You are merely its keeper."

"Merely its keeper," Raela repeated. "Yet this distinction comes with great responsibility and sacrifice."

"Everyone in the tribe has their place," the elder replied. "Perhaps you were undeserving of yours. Now, where is it?"

Cheeks aflame and temper flaring, Raela decided to spread her anger and provoke the elder by revealing what she'd bottled inside herself over many days. Admitting her crime would keep him from invading her person, which his nearing hands looked inclined to do, and would also keep him from discovering the extra padding that had filled around her waistline.

"I don't have it," she said.

"Where did you put it?" he asked, nudging her travel bag with his free hand.

"I left it behind," she replied, swiveling from his reach.

"Where?" The elder looked past her as if expecting to see it somewhere behind them.

"No," she told him, "I did not leave it in a tunnel."

"Then where is it? In a different cavern? We need it here with us. Already we are starting to feel"—he paused and wrinkled his nose—"different. It's quite unsettling."

"The reason you feel that way is because I left it in the forest beneath a tree."

The elder's face paled as her words registered. With horror in his eyes, he finally spoke, "What tree? Why would you do such a thing?"

A lie would only prolong the future gossip, so she told him.

"I left it for Rebial."

"Stupid woman!" He raised his arm as if to slap her and probably would have had the midwife not stepped in from the tunnel.

"She is with child," the midwife told him. "And she's the granddaughter of the seer."

Very conscious of stone walls entrapping her within the moment, Raela's emotions soared like never before in her entire life. She felt anger at the midwife for revealing her secret without permission, relief that the unborn child inside her belly may save her from being slapped, guilt if this were the case, since she did not wish to use an innocent child to her advantage.

"She is with child?" The elder squinted at her belly then gave her a wary once over. Resigned, he said, "Of course, she is. The other women grow thin, yet our distraught scribe continues to grow round."

He placed his head in his hands momentarily, slid them down his face before clenching them to his chest as if to keep himself from hitting her.

Face burning, Raela refused to make eye contact with the midwife despite the woman's attempt to prevent the violence against her.

"And so that is your reward, granddaughter of the seer?" The elder leaned in close, a devilish look in his eyes.

Raela flinched and stepped back.

"You betray the entire tribe, and yet your baby will be spared." His words were spoken quietly despite having lethal undertones. "You do know what this means for us, don't you? Remember the passage? Not a generation will pass for those who possess the prophecy. Well, we no longer possess the prophecy, so guess what? Only death awaits us down here. We will never see the sun again."

This time the elder did strike her, hard against the cheek. She raised a hand to her swollen face, furious at his trespass. But her tears uniting with the birthmark on her thumb—the mark of the scribe—gave her strength. Somehow it tempered the burn.

"Surely Rebial will realize his mistake and try to find us," she said. "He knows of the book's importance."

The midwife stood between them now, but Raela knew the woman's protection was no match for the elder's wrath if he so wished to deploy it.

"Let me tell you something," the elder said condescendingly. "Let me tell you how you have erred. For your fickle love, you have given up your future."

"No, Rebial is my future. I cannot exist only as a tool of the tribe. I am a person, a woman."

"Yes, a woman," the elder continued with the same mocking tone. "Pining for a mate who does not love you in return. Before you were a scribe, a leader of our people. Now you are only a fool who is also a woman."

The elder turned away from her to walk farther into the cavern. He placed a hand against the stone wall and bent forward, presumably to collect his thoughts. The torch he held with his other hand burned low, casting a brooding shadow on the wall.

Tears gushed down Raela's face. "How could he speak to me like that?" she whispered to the midwife, voice wobbling.

"He is not concerned with your feelings," the midwife replied. "And now I am wondering whether I should be too."

Raela froze and stared. "But you cannot desert me. I have no one left."

"That is the path you chose by making the decision that you did."

"Don't you think he will come for me?"

"I do not have faith in someone who owns little faith himself. His pride is too strong. And besides, there may come a time when it is too late to alter his decision."

Raela shook with sobs.

"At any rate," the midwife said. "You have to live with what you decided, and I am a firm believer in life."

"Is that supposed to make me feel better?" she asked.

Before the midwife could respond, the elder righted himself suddenly and strode back over with urgent steps.

With the fiery eyes of a madman, he asked, "Where are you leading us?"

"What do you mean?" she said, fear tightening her muscles.

"Where are you leading us in these tunnels without the book to guide you?"

"To our destination," she replied.

"How do you know that you are leading us correctly?"

"Because I memorized it before we left," she replied.

"So you planned ahead for this?"

By his expression, she knew her answer would make matters worse.

"Yes," she whispered.

"Did your grandfather know of this planned betrayal?"

She did not bother defending herself, more concerned with the reputation of her grandfather. "Of course not."

The elder roughly grabbed onto her forearm. "We must tell them," he said fiendishly, handing the midwife the torch. Then he wrenched Raela from the cavern to where the others waited.

⋍

Vandor listened eagerly to the muffled sounds of distress that echoed from the cavern. He and his clan from the east hovered behind the western tribe, waiting for their chance to move in on Raela's misfortune.

Torches burned all around them as they endured the stifling wait. The persecution of their reluctant and now disreputable leader had been long in coming.

It was well known now that she had denied a distraught mother's request to view the prophecy. He assumed, as did everyone, that she was being reprimanded for that. The whispers confirmed most agreed with this punishment—even Raela's mother. Strangely, the woman showed no outward fondness for her daughter after what she'd done. And by the way the scene was carrying on inside the cavern, somewhat shielded within stone walls, even more would be revealed when they emerged.

Why else had the midwife not been thrown out after invading the space?

Vandor had been waiting for this moment since he'd seen Raela's small hand resting on her stomach in that nurturing sort of way that soon-to-be mothers had.

The western tribe still had no idea. He inwardly shook his head at these sorry souls who did not pay attention to the clues that were so obvious to someone like himself. They were like children, so trusting without using their minds to think, so different than the members of his clan who now clustered tightly around him. He'd been whispering to them the truth for days now. They hoped that Raela's baby would distract her from her duties with the book.

"Wait until they throw her out," he hissed to them, his words barely audible over the din coming from the cavern, "and the rest rebuke her. Then while she is in tears and wallowing in her misery, we will relieve her of at least one of her burdens. Perhaps ask her to join us."

Still, he would be diplomatic.

It is your right as the book's keeper to decide who sees it, he would say. *If you come with us, you will maintain that right.*

Or perhaps when the main tribe ostracized her, she would become a willing member. This was the preferred scenario by many of the more sympathetic members of his clan.

Once they had her as their ally, he was certain they

could distance themselves from the western tribe. Their warriors could no longer even be identified, so weak they'd all become.

The sounds grew closer. The elder stormed from the cavern, dragging Raela by the arm. He stood before them as a mountain of fury. She sniffled beside him, tearful and distraught. But instead of throwing her aside, he called for their attention.

"Come listen to what our so-called leader has done." His voice shook with wrath.

Vandor cocked his head. What was the reason for the elder's tone? This was not how he'd supposed Raela's pregnancy would be called out in front of everyone. Many partook in the act; it was the consequence that most avoided. The elder's demeanor seemed unusually cruel for a bit of public humiliation.

Either way, someone dejected was easier to bring to your side than someone who was within the favor of the masses. Whatever was about to transpire would only work in the favor of his clan.

"Tell them," the elder commanded, once the others had convened tightly around them.

Vandor and his clan stayed at the outskirts.

"You tell them," Raela retorted, almost as if she had the spirit of her lover.

And in a way, she did, for Vandor was certain that the child was his.

"This woman," the elder spat out, "our tribal scribe, is not the respected granddaughter of our past seer that we assumed her to be. Not only is she pregnant, but she is also a traitor. She left the prophecy behind. For her lover, the father of her child."

Gasps erupted from the crowd as the elder seethed before them.

Raela tried to yank her arm away but remained unable to free herself from the elder's tight grasp. "Rebial will come," she protested. "He will bring it to us. I know he will."

Vandor's mouth fell open. He became dizzy. Whispers grew heavy, like a swarm of insects. He remembered then that he loathed insects, for they were hard to study. Despite this, he grew even more aggravated, for their familiar buzz was a sound he had not heard for some time.

Some grumbled harsh insults. Others wailed with anguish.

"How do we know she's leading us to the correct place?" someone asked.

"She should have given us the book and stayed behind with him."

"We should kill her," someone said.

"No," the elder snapped impatiently, "we cannot kill her. And I will tell you why. She has memorized the words in the book. She has memorized the map. Only she knows the way. This she has done to protect herself."

His words settled grotesquely as a realization surfaced. She had consciously betrayed them. She had not suffered from the madness of a woman in grief when she'd left the book behind.

Tempers rose, aligned with the flames of torches scattered in the crowd.

"How dare she flaunt her pregnancy like that after what happened to the more respectable women in our tribe."

"She's put our whole tribe in jeopardy, defying the will of nature just like her lover."

Amid the barrage of angry accusations, the elder released

Raela's arm and stepped aside, forcing her to endure the outrage and ridicule all alone.

But she did not lower her gaze in shame. She merely stood and took it all in with a glare that would compete with Rebial's if he were present.

Vandor backed away until he felt rough stone press against him. He shared the same agony as those around him—the loss of a life-giving book.

His clan from the east had been prepared to break away from the rest to begin a different way of life—one where curiosity was not frowned upon or reviled. They had aspired to dominate the animal kingdom as opposed to cooperating with it. Advance themselves and pursue lofty goals instead of just meandering through life and accepting what was offered. There was no reason to obey the laws of nature like beasts, using their brains for the benefit of all when they were not all on even ground.

But so they would until the time came to reemerge. His clan would wait underground with the rest until redemption came. But this redemption would now only come to their descendants. It would never be theirs to embrace.

He refrained from sharing even a glance with any of his clansmen. It would only expel disappointment, and he was certain they were already experiencing much of their own.

Raela glowered before them, her tears falling as swiftly as his hope.

So this would be the way he ended. His back pressed against cold stone. No way for his curiosity to be quenched. Nothing to study or examine. He would die a man in perpetual yearning for something greater than time would allow him.

Perhaps if he trolled the passages, he would find something to study, some eyeless fish or lowly insect clinging to the ceiling. This would be how he spent the rest of his existence—lurking, waiting, searching for something meager to watch die.

CHAPTER TWENTY-SEVEN

TREMORS STIRRED THE memory of a forgotten night-mare—one Rebial could barely solidify inside his thoughts now laced with brush and wood. Mycelium alerted roots that sent messages to trees. They bent to listen. He picked up on the danger as it traveled through the dirt.

Something catastrophic was happening, something bigger than just a man or two chopping a few trunks. He sensed the onset of another war. The giant beasts had returned. This time he would get there before they wreaked the same destruction.

With the mental focus of a warrior, he melted in and out of his surroundings as he traveled through the woods. The big cats loped alongside him in a physical sense, matching his speed. He passed through dirt and crags, leaves and wood, a plethora of different organisms, until finally he emerged near where the giant beasts had rolled in.

The pandemonium he encountered was greater than everything that had come before.

They were destroying the area alongside the desolation they'd so recently left behind. Grass and undergrowth had begun to grow back, and some of the smaller animals had returned, but Rebial knew it would be a long time before the area fully healed. The wound was almost as devastating as the one that had killed his father.

Enlarging the wound wouldn't help.

The strange beasts were wasting no time. Giant claws ripped trees from the ground as if they were blades of grass. His enemies huddled nearby, wearing yellow war helmets, directing the movements of the beasts. One man sat within the head of the beast, directing the claws based on gestures men made at ground level.

More strange beasts were rolling in, crushing whatever was unlucky enough to be in their way. He would stop them before they destroyed everything.

He rushed forward to avenge, sidestepped a falling ancestor before it crushed him. Nearing a giant beast, with stealth not yet noticed by the men, for he blended in so easily, he raised a spear to attack. But the beast's strange smell burned his nostrils. He touched its yellow body and leaned in close. Something thrummed inside its compact skin, but it was not the beating of a heart.

Pressing the point of his spear against it only made a scratch. These beasts were impenetrable. Not made of flesh, they were as lifeless as the spear inside his hand—manmade objects that merely mimicked giant beasts. And so he could not kill them.

Another ancestor shook the ground as Rebial fell back and dropped his spear, still as invisible to the invaders as the soul of the wood. And how was it something without a soul could destroy the life force of his forest? What travesty was this?

As he watched the chaos ensue—men directing soulless beasts to destroy life—his emotions fought a battle inside him. The magnitude of what he was up against shook him as the ground trembled. And something inside him snapped just as viciously.

There was only one way to stop so many of them at once. It would not suffice to take them one by one, not when they controlled such giant weapons. Suddenly he knew a better way as a potent idea formed.

He would inspire the trees to avenge themselves. His pride told him he had the power to do it. He would kill them all. The thought enlivened him, caused his body to impulsively jerk forward, but something still held him back—a tiny flicker in his mind that may have been doubt. He would squash this too.

Another ancestor fell in the seconds he spent collecting his thoughts. He would not allow these evil parasites to kill one more.

He stirred the insects from the vegetation and their hidden haunts. They flew in swarms to overtake and mar the vision of the intruders.

Arms flailing, his enemies erratically shifted their whereabouts.

Now was the time to put his plan of attack into action. If he could imagine it, then the trees would obey him. And so he unleashed his hate into the wood.

Directing his anger downward, Rebial became one with the roots. He spread himself thinner and thinner as he expanded into their winding network. Commanded by his mind, they pried themselves free.

Treetops wavered, their union with the soil now broken. Ancient trees creaked like unused bones as their roots ripped from the ground. The world fell all around as giant trunks landed with a deafening crash onto beasts and parasites alike. The intruders stopped moving, crushed in heaping piles beneath giant shards of bark.

Particles of wood and bits of leaves clouded the air, filling the unnatural silence that came after. Satisfaction brimming, Rebial breathed in the woodsy scent of his reward.

But then the dust settled. A pile of light debris started moving. One man wriggled out from beneath it, having evaded the heavy onslaught. Seeing Rebial when he climbed free, in all his greenness and knobby limbs—for there was nothing to blend into anymore—his eyes widened.

He backed away in terror, turned to run but stopped short when he saw a cougar perched nearby. Its dignified pose within the rubble unhinged the man further.

He looked around wildly, saw a giant beast that had been largely dented by a fallen trunk. He tried to scramble up its yellow side, but like Rebial's spear, his nails only scratched the surface.

There was nothing left for this man in the world, so Rebial would show him how a warrior sealed his victory. Darting forward, he dragged his own sharply whittled fingers down the man's chest. Body split open, the man fell to his knees. His face smashed onto a waiting stump. Like the rest of his companions, he wouldn't move again.

A giant beast began rumbling at the edge of the destruction. Another man was inside. He gave Rebial a frightened look before he and his giant beast blasted forward and away. They left behind an unsavory odor within a trail of smoke.

Rebial considered following, using his powers to tilt the trees to stop them from proceeding, but thought better of it.

His father had always said to be sure that someone from the opposing side remained. It was a strategy that ensured the men back home would hear of the danger. It was a strategy that would ensure these other men would stay behind.

Isn't this why they kept coming back? He'd been hiding his kills too well. Allowing a survivor this time meant that no one would return.

He turned away from the retreating enemy, looked at the piles of death all around him, and tried to find happiness in the method he'd used to win the war. Half of the trees that would have been killed remained. But now, in the aftermath, he instead found his satisfaction waning—as if his leftover impression matched his injured forest.

The feeling was strangely familiar. Except this time, he had caused it. And like the man he had so recently killed, he fell to his knees in despair of what he'd done.

CHAPTER TWENTY-EIGHT

HIS ABSENCE STALKED her through the tunnels. The cave's suffocating, cold walls reminded her that solitude was now her lone companion. She walked stiffly behind the others, keeping her distance. They had not allowed her to join them ever since she'd confessed to leaving behind the book. Once she instructed them where to go next, they forced her to follow as if she deserved to be behind them instead of this being her choice all along.

Despite their scorn, she remained a good leader by continuing to show them the way.

Her betrayal had been necessary, she kept reminding herself, to stay true to all she deemed important. Namely, her love for her husband. And the recognition that she was her own person and not a tool. But what was Rebial's sacrifice to her?

It seemed clear that, so far, his only sacrifice was to the woods.

Now that they were nearing their destination, during which she had endured so much, a strange melancholy came over her. She felt an insatiable urge to write.

So after dutifully sending the tribe ahead of her and

making sure no one was watching, she dug in her travel bag for her writing utensil. The words came as if they were separate from her thoughts or perhaps straight from her heart.

Writing utensil in hand, her fingers danced across the stone.

The words poured from her soul, much like they had the day she'd written down the prophecy for her grandfather. Her message was pure poetry, she realized upon rereading it. Perhaps it would even propel Rebial further into action.

Once he made it this far, there was no turning back, and he would likely be feeling just a bit hesitant. His once invincible pride would be bruised. He would be expecting to join a woman glad to see him. Yet she was not so desperate that his stubbornness would be ignored.

The words she'd written on the cave's wall implied this. She did not regret them.

Perhaps if he thought that she had given up on him, he would arrive in a humble manner, looking for forgiveness.

Ruminating over his actions had been her reality for too many days to count. She was not normally a woman to inject those around her with the drama that ensued from her emotions, yet she was ready to share this burden with her lover.

She was also ready to share the joy of birthing a child.

So while she wanted him to come to her with some regrets and perhaps even a bit of shame, he also needed to realize that he would be forgiven once he arrived.

She reread the passage, proud of herself for the artfulness of her words. Carefully pulling the turquoise bead that represented hope from her travel bag, she placed it on the ledge jutting from the wall.

He would see the bead and know what the gesture

meant. And perhaps both it and her message would cause him to hurry even faster.

◈

Rebial stumbled back the way he'd come. Finding a hollowed trunk whose darkness beckoned, he crawled inside. His place of rest was now the forest when he grew tired, for he no longer desired the comfort of a padded bed. He found more solace cradled in wood.

He settled into the damp pocket, breathed in its dank scent.

Regardless of his change in habit, he would continue to protect the village as if it were a living memory from his past. His preferred method of comfort would not affect this. And comfort was something he deeply craved.

For even though he had conquered the men and his splintered body remained unscathed from the attack, Rebial felt ill. The sounds of trees ripping from the dirt, by his command, tormented him. And he was disgusted with himself for committing such treason.

He had killed the men, but in exchange, too many trees had met death as well. The effectiveness of his method did not negate this unsettling truth. He would have to use a different tactic from now on, go back to his old ways, if any man dared step foot inside his woods again.

For what was the point of staying behind to avenge the wood if he had to go so far as to treat it just as wickedly as his enemy? If his tactics matched the ones he was trying to prevent? If his strategy caused him to feel the pain he would rather avoid?

Before, he'd felt as if a chunk had been removed from his own body. At present, a gaping hole resided in his heart.

And now that he had time to think, it occurred to him that there'd been other signs that something was askew. For causing trees to fall was not a tactic he would have readily implemented at the start. It was as if he had circled back around to the place he'd been before, disturbed again by an entire portion of his woods destroyed, except now he was the reason for it.

As he killed, and though he remained unharmed, something inside him had changed during the days in which a lone tree fell here or there. For of course he'd had to allow some trees to fall since these men were sometimes chopping in different places at once. As long as he could direct the trunks which direction to fall, he'd felt as if he had won.

But these fallen trees, and the blood that came after, only added to a creeping sensation that refined itself over time. More and more of the invaders' blood kept seeping into the soil.

The more blood that spilled in his forest, the more he lusted for it. When it seeped into the dirt, he felt as if it soaked into his skin.

And he supposed the invaders' flesh rotting inside the woods could be infecting the nature of the forest. So was it possible their rot was starting to infect his mind as well?

Is this why he had chosen such a destructive strategy, one that had ultimately ruined a portion of what he had vowed to protect? Is this what his father and the prophecy had meant when they said these evil parasitic men were like a disease? Had they infected him to the point that his own tactics used to counter theirs had become infected too? Hence the broken woods he'd left behind.

He felt sick, but not with cold or fever. It had been a

gradual thing, building until he had committed this horrible act that now made him question everything.

He scrambled to come up with a way that would have been just as effective, wiped out both the invaders and their giant soulless objects without suffering the same effects, but came up short.

He could have spun in and out of nature, killing them. But for some reason, an evil had corrupted him, and he had used the forest as a weapon. Killing something to protect it made no sense, and he realized then how far he'd gone astray.

Could he be fixed or was he too damaged? Would he have to wait until the forest recovered over hundreds of years to feel the same? Since he surely could not withstand this length of time, did this mean he was tainted forever?

Either way, wanting to feel the same was unrealistic since he was not the same. He was sure of this. For better or worse, he had become almost too connected to the woods. His freedom to merge in and out upon his whim had jeopardized his freedom as a man.

But if he was no longer a man, did it even matter?

CHAPTER TWENTY-NINE

WHILE RAELA LAGGED behind in the passageways, buried in thoughts about Rebial and the child growing inside her belly, the rest of the tribe remained focused on the path ahead.

Their persistent mumblings echoed back at her, lined the blurry edges of the tunnels. She understood their mindset quite well.

Looking to the past was a hindrance. It was detrimental not only to their state of minds, but also the purpose at hand. Remembering what had happened before only caused suffering—pain over the loss of their home, the loss of their children, the loss of their old way of life. Some mourned the sun. Others yearned for a scenic view. The life they lived now only contained grayish darkness, clay and dirt, the color brown that never went away.

Not everyone was coping well. Some were wildly disoriented, walking the tunnels with their hands pressed onto its walls as if afraid that they would fall. Some grew claustrophobic, crawling at times as they longed for open space. Raela ignored them, for she had her own troubles to bear. Yet she knew that some blamed her for their madness, for if the prophecy were with them, its rays of hope would have kept them sane. So they claimed, but she had her doubts.

Nevertheless, they continued on. It wasn't until they grew close to their destination, that Raela was allowed to lead from a position up front. They followed attentively but not closely, which is much what she preferred.

So when she came to a series of stone ledges that ascended to an opening outlined in stone, she knew this was the entrance to the cavern that would be their final resting space.

She stepped inside with her torch lit, glad to have a brief moment to herself to view the new surroundings. The chamber before her was vast and extraordinary, though not in the way they were accustomed.

Their village was now a maze-like rocky outcropping that jutted intricately from the ground. Pools of shimmering water rimmed its exterior walls. What appeared to be a garden grew unnaturally from cracks in stone. She tried not to overanalyze these mysteries of life in such a bleak space, for the prophecy indicated all their needs would be met.

Crystals hung from the ceiling in strange and perplexing patterns, beautifying what was otherwise a desolate cavern deep underground. They no longer had stars to view, nor celestial bodies in the sky, but would have to satisfy themselves with what was nice to look at inside a cave.

She sensed that even having reached it, they would still spend their days looking forward, fantasizing about their children or grandchildren being lucky enough to reemerge. Being hopeful it would happen before too much time had passed. Perhaps before their own deaths.

A tribal elder drifted in then and stopped beside her.

"This is our destination," Raela said. "This is our new home."

He curled his lip and glanced about. "So this is where I will die then." He walked further into the wide cavern, holding his torch overhead.

The rest of the tribe trickled out of the tunnel, one by one, filling the outskirts of the chamber with various expressions on their faces. Some glared at Raela as they walked past, apparently of the same opinion as the elder. Others gazed with awe at the glittering beauty of their new sky. Still others were hesitant, uncertain, and hung back near the entrance.

Raela placed a hand on her round belly as she stared at the wide expanse, deciding that if she were to die here, then perhaps that would not be such a bad thing. Her surroundings were picturesque in their own way, now that she had accepted them, and the area itself rivaled the size of their old village.

She choked back a sudden sob at the remembrance, placed a hand over her mouth to keep the others from noticing her moment of vulnerability. It grew harder each day to keep her emotions in check now that she carried a child.

There was no sun, but that hadn't seemed to matter so much in a physical way since the babies had been stolen. Most specifically once Nola's baby had been stolen. Raela shuddered and hugged her stomach tighter. The worst had already happened. Now all they had to do was wait and hope Rebial would join them.

She still held onto that hope. Someday, she was certain, he would make his way here. Her grandfather said she had the sight after all.

Something inside the stone village beckoned her away from the others. She walked past the milling crowd, past the tribal members, who by now were chatting amongst themselves and pointing at intricately shaped stalactites hanging from the ceiling.

The tribal elder who remained the bane of her existence followed, not close, but she could sense him keeping pace behind. She walked into their new village. Small rooms lined its winding pathway. With a little ingenuity, these carved-out areas would make for good housing.

She wound farther and farther through the curved path, into the village's interior. She walked longer than she felt she should have to walk, based on her impression of its size outside the walls. Her heart pounded as she neared what drew her. Anxiety compounded in her body with each step forward.

Entering a large, round room with a floor pieced together with chunks of stone, she saw what loomed inside. An opening with edges that protruded up to her waist was its centerpiece. Waves of heat billowed out. As she neared, sweat formed instantaneously. She peered over the edge, her whole face now burning. There was nothing to see but an eerie yet tantalizing darkness.

It was the kind of darkness that contained all kinds of things, which made it all the more intriguing.

Curious about its depths, she pulled a small bead from her bag, tossed it over the edge and waited. But there was no faint plunk of a landing in response. The silence stretched on and on until she gave up thinking there would ever be a sound. Yet the lack of sound was telling, suggesting the hole went farther into the planet than she could fathom. She knew then this was where she was to lay to rest the prophecy, once Rebial brought it to her.

Power resonated from the hole, oozing from an unseen force. Its effects were all-encompassing and gave her further insight.

Something resided inside this hole, something quite unstable. This unsettling feeling differed from how she'd felt during her final days inside the forest. It was not the thumping of an intruder walking where they did not belong. This came from deeper inside the planet than she could possibly imagine or had ever bothered to imagine before.

The source was stronger, genuine and real, more dynamic even. It did not signal worse times to come but merely overwhelmed her with its presence.

There was something more to what remained invisible inside. Somehow, she knew that she had done something important. She had made a choice that was neither good nor bad. Her fate had yet to be decided. The brewing pot of emotions beneath her—this unknown entity expelling wafts of heat—was thinking, mulling, considering her.

She had not brought the prophecy like she'd been expected to do, but perhaps there was still time. Something still hung in the balance. Truth and consequence hovered precariously together on the line that forever separated right from wrong.

"Is this where the prophecy should be placed?" the elder asked upon his tentative approach.

He looked over the side with uncharacteristic meekness.

Raela wiped damp hair behind her ears. "Yes," she said. "We need to cover it immediately. Until we can place the prophecy in it."

"The prophecy that will never arrive?" the elder asked sarcastically. He backed away as if to keep his disrespect aimed only at her and not whatever resided in the opening.

"No," she replied, "the one that Rebial will return to us once he realizes the error of his ways."

"Foolish girl. A man as proud as him never realizes the error of his ways."

His comment jabbed at her like a heel loosening rocks upon a cliff. On the verge of crumbling before him, she stood strong and kept her ground.

"He will come for me," she insisted. "Neither he nor the prophecy will remain forever in the forest."

"The only thing I'm certain of when it comes to forever," the elder replied dryly, "is that's how long the covering we place upon that wicked opening will remain."

"We'll remove it," she said simply, "when Rebial joins us."

She moved away from it then before he could consider tossing her inside.

Perhaps if she were lucky, the odd presence would take him. But he quickly joined her through the winding stone, overtook her and kept going as if he feared the same outcome.

CHAPTER THIRTY

HIS SKIN WAS rough like bark, his hair a wispy mess of matted vegetation. He moved from tree to tree as if they shared the same body. He could take on the nature of any one of them, transform into the beast it vaguely resembled or remain a lone tree with the purpose of existing as part of the whole.

He could be wherever he set his mind to being. This is how he wafted in and out so successfully. The mere focus of a thought could place him anywhere he chose.

Sometimes he remembered he was a man and sometimes not, irrespective of whether he retained his true shape or was flirting between the shape of many things. His thoughts were different though his motives had meshed with that of the forest's. No longer a bystander, he was now connected to everything, and everything was also now a part of him.

He could run swiftly as a deer, prowl as stealthily as a cougar. He could burrow in the soil like a gopher or a worm. He could see through the eyes of an insect many miles away.

So it was out of desperation to remember who he truly was that he decided to record his lingering memory of himself within the husk of a tree—nearby the one whose canopy he used to sit in with his human lover. Despite the threat of the prophecy hanging over their head, life was much simpler then.

He ducked into the rotted trunk and used a splintery finger to etch words into the bark.

The wood entraps me. I cannot break free. We are attached and grow united. By the wood's design I am no longer a man, but I remain Rebial.

Just recording the thought put him at ease, for it was now ingrained within his mind just the same as it was embedded into the forest. He could refer to it at will. It would be his last sliver of a reminder that there was something else linked to his existence. If he had a name, then he was not all forest. Remembering this would slow the delirium that had begun creeping into what remained of his humanity.

The clomping sound of the elder restlessly pacing outside their stone village infuriated the midwife. She stood with her back to the outer wall, arms crossed over her chest. Her face creased with worry as she pondered his last remark.

We should kill the child she smears in our faces.

He'd said the damning sentence with only a slight frown. She had rebuked him. Still, he would not give up, had only looked regretful for one moment before he spoke again.

"We cannot let her bear the child," he insisted.

His heartlessness disgusted her.

"How would we stop it?" she asked. "We are not a culture that kills innocent babies. Besides, we have experienced enough of that type of grief."

"That is exactly why we cannot allow it. More deserving women have been robbed of their offspring."

"That fault is the prophecy's, and the prophecy's alone," she replied. "Are you questioning its wisdom?"

"Shouldn't I?" the elder asked bitterly. "Look who it chose as its keeper."

The midwife did not respond, having also suffered from the same thought. Having decided not to voice this out loud, she would not allow the elder to provoke more doubt.

"Either way," he said, "she is a traitor, and her child should not be spared. Give her the plant that terminates a pregnancy."

The midwife startled at his boldness, placed a hand over her heart.

"You think we elders don't know about it?" he asked, noticing her surprised look. "Just because such a thing is not openly discussed does not mean women don't share such stories in secret."

Of course, she knew how most women were—gossipy, always looking for a scandal, battling inside themselves on whether to reveal a secret. Though men were not innocent of such things either.

Still, she would not bend and agree with his unconscionable suggestion.

"I cannot force an expectant mother to eat it," she replied. "Nor will I deceive one and be the reason she loses a child."

The elder threw up his hands. "She must suffer for her actions in some way. She cannot betray the tribe and avoid punishment."

But the midwife had sympathy for Raela, having been in love once, when she, herself, was a young woman. Before her lot in life had been decided for her. Once her skills with herbs had become known, the tribe had designated her its midwife. She would care for the children of other women but never her own. This truth only added to her compassion, for she knew how it felt to devote your life to only serving others.

"I refuse to be the reason why another woman never sees her child grow up," she said. "Your demand is too cruel. For all involved. Besides that, it's counterproductive. She will never reveal what she has memorized if—"

"She will tell us once her child is gone and she has nothing left," the elder insisted.

"I refuse to be responsible for this. Her betrayal of the tribe was an act of passion."

"Acts of passion aren't premeditated," the elder countered.

"She still believes her lover will come."

The midwife could see this hope on Raela's face every time she encountered the woman.

"He won't come, and we both know it," he snarled. "So we will do as I proposed."

The midwife inwardly fumed.

"It would be better," the elder added slowly, "if you were the one who gave it to her. More humane even."

He gave her an unsettling stare to emphasize his meaning. "She trusts you."

This was exactly why the midwife did not want to get involved. Yet this responsibility she must bear if she wanted what was best for the tribe.

"Perhaps it would be better," she agreed slowly, "to be treated by a gentler hand."

The elder perked up, relaxing his rigid stance. "So you've brought the plant?" he asked.

"Of course," the midwife said. "I brought it to prevent what happened in the tunnels even though it was too late to be of any use. I will go offer it to her now."

The elder's eyes gleamed with hope as she turned her back on him to enter the stone village.

Entering the maze, she walked past dwellings filled sparsely with people until she reached her own. She dug through her meager belongings, found the plant the elder had directed her to give the poor young woman and prepared it for consumption.

Then she wound through the passageways to Raela's dwelling, which was situated closest to the odd opening at the center. The younger woman sat by herself in the small enclosure, staring at the wall in a way that the midwife found disturbing. This was not a woman she wished to unhinge even a fraction more. Even an inch this way or that could be the tipping point that might result in disaster.

No matter what the elder thought, the tribe needed Raela. And so would the child that would burst from her belly any day now.

Still, it was her duty to carry out the elder's wishes.

❧

Even though she could hear others nearby, for sounds echoed generously inside their village, Raela felt vastly alone. Above her, crystals sparkled like stars. She missed the stars.

More specifically, she missed gazing at them with Rebial, snuggled together in the treetops.

The tribe's environment was now framed in stone, much different from the open sky and rich vegetation that had once surrounded them. Each family had a small enclosure in which to finish living out their existence. Many gritted their teeth at this reality. They did not fail to remind Raela this bleak ending for their tribe was all her fault.

Hearing a subtle knocking near the rugged opening that served as her doorway, she looked up. The midwife stood there, something odd belaboring her expression.

"I have brought you a gift," said the midwife, stepping into the tiny room. She held out her hand. Small leaves and chunks of an unfamiliar plant rested in her palm. Yet her arm shook unsteadily.

Raela stared at the midwife in disbelief. Suspicion crept in soon after. Most people when giving gifts had a lightness in their face, a gleeful anticipation that they would soon be giving pleasure to the recipient. Instead, the midwife's face held an uncertainty, a foreboding even, as if she were not glad to be giving anything.

Could it be because of Raela's current standing in the tribe? The midwife was giving her the herb to be kind, yet still struggled with directing this kindness at someone so controversial?

Or perhaps the midwife gave the gift out of duty? This seemed more likely. Yet who delegated this duty? Did it come from the obligation of a midwife or an elder's vindictive whim?

One option was more believable than the other. The half-smile faded from Raela's face. "What is it?"

"An herb that many women before you have taken for their pregnancies," the midwife replied cryptically.

But Raela would not be so easily fooled. "What does it do?"

"It's not what it does that you need to concern yourself with. I can brew it into a tea for you. Or," she added, "I can say I gave it to you, and you can use it as you wish."

Suddenly she knew what this hesitant gift was all about. And perhaps her grandfather was correct in saying she had the gift of sight.

"I see," Raela nodded, taking in the subtle clue. "You were told to give it to me, which can only mean one thing."

"There's no need for this discussion when you can just take it and be done," the midwife said quickly. "Take it in your hand I mean."

"But not by mouth?" Raela asked.

"That's up to you. I'm just doing what was asked of me."

"I won't take it at all, how's that? By mouth or hand. And you can tell the elder I am too smart for his petty games."

"If you are as smart as you say, then you would be aware that brash defiance is not always the best tactic," the midwife replied, finally dropping all pretenses.

"Then I will be stern instead," Raela said, "even though I already have a plan and it is foolproof. But if I choose to be defiant, there is nothing he can do."

"I hope you are right, my dear, for the elders' hearts have turned to stone with things not going as they'd planned. They would think nothing of forcing the herb down your throat."

Raela shuddered at the thought.

"The threat of that cajoled me to make the offering to begin with. I would never on my own accord. I cannot help you. I can, however, do things my own way."

The midwife placed the herbs on the floor beside Raela, who gathered them back up and handed the mixture back to her.

"I appreciate that, midwife. It is the true gift in this encounter. Come and watch me show an elder that he is not as clever as he believes himself to be."

"I will watch from afar. Where it is safe."

"If Rebial were here," Raela said, using the wall for support as she slowly stood, "we would both be safe no matter where we were standing."

The midwife looked away briefly, then said, "The elder scoffs that you are only a woman. I hope you show him what that entails."

For someone who liked to pretend she was a neutral bystander and not a friend, the midwife always managed to encourage, albeit in a backhanded kind of way. Perhaps it was her way of maintaining her loyalty to the rest of the tribe.

"I will show him," Raela said as she exited the small space.

⚶

Raela stepped from the stone village, shoulders back so her belly protruded without shame. The elder stood just outside it, staring up at the crystals like he, at one time, may have stared at stars. She was disgusted that he was partaking in such an act of reflection while he sent the midwife to do his dirty work. It also bothered her that she had recently been doing the same thing.

"I will not eat the plant that will kill my child," she said, defiance edging her voice despite her best intentions.

The elder glared at the midwife who had followed after all, but she only stared back evenly. Her look seemed to say that he would not make her feel guilt for doing her job of sustaining life.

Raela found inspiration in the midwife's stubbornness. It reminded her of Rebial. Still, she didn't want the woman to suffer for her choice like she had suffered for her own.

"The midwife offered me a plant that I know quite well already," Raela lied. "I will not be so easily fooled."

"What makes you think you have a choice?" the elder said, leering at her.

Raela did not waver. "Because only I know the secret route back to the surface that our people must travel."

"You think that gives you power?"

"It gives me strength. But I won't live forever. And I may not live long enough to see us reemerge. But my child may. Or hers. And she is the only one I care to relay these facts to."

He slumped forward as he stared at her, though his posture did not match his angry expression.

"You cannot kill my child," Raela said again, voice rising, "for I will pass my information to her. If you destroy either one of us, all memory of the prophecy will be lost. And it will be a blind future for not only you but for your children as well. And the tribe's."

The elder eyed her shrewdly while the midwife hid her smile. "You have become quite the defiant one," he said, "influenced by your lover."

Tears threatened her cheeks at his mention, more impactful than the elder's disdain. "That is not the correct word. Enlightened by him is more accurate. Rebial may have been wrong about the significance of the prophecy, but he was correct in his opinion of the integrity of our elders."

"This descent has been hard on all of us, no matter what you believe," the elder grumbled.

"But perhaps if you'd been willing to make him a warrior, give him his final wish, he would be here now. And so would the prophecy."

The elder shook his head, unwilling to accept his part

in fate. "There was no point in making him a warrior. Look around you. Trapped inside this cave, it would have confused his spirit. Although by now, I'm sure, he is only a spirit."

But Raela refused to fathom he could be correct. Rebial still lived. How else would he bring them the book?

CHAPTER THIRTY-ONE

WHEN THE PAINS came, Raela knew not only that the time had come, but that no one would rush to help her. Months ago, the midwife had stated she would not. Her mother had not forgiven her, did not even check in on her condition, and therefore the midwife would have no one begging her conscience for aid.

Raela would surely not ask for aid herself, for her pride had become just as stubborn as Rebial's with his child inside her. Besides, no one wanted to give birth with a pillar of resentment standing nearby.

A sharp and sudden pain refocused her thoughts, so debilitating and severe that it froze her in place. Her breath at first came through in a strangled choke as she forbade herself from crying out. Yet she calmed herself by remembering to align her breath with the pains. She concentrated on the energy flowing in and out of her body as she inhaled and exhaled. The pain became tolerable then, and she grew confident that she could birth her child alone.

Clutching her stomach, she knelt onto the cold, hard floor. She laid a blanket down and then herself atop it. She formed a picture of Rebial inside her mind—focused solely on his fierceness, his confidence, his pride. Remembering him is how she would bear it. She directed her thoughts so fully that she even envisioned him standing nearby, was certain he could feel her thoughts upon him above ground, wherever he was inside the forest.

Unless he had obeyed her wishes after all. He may even be coming toward her in the tunnels.

Her smile turned into a look of horror at the sharpness of her next contraction. No, this child only allowed her to think of itself, would not let her be distracted.

She forced her breaths to be slow and steady like she had practiced. Pain came and went and lingered until she thought she would cry out. Time was no longer something she could measure, but a space filled with giant bouts of agony and only lapses of relief.

The only desire she now had was to force this child from her body. She could feel her baby edging toward its entrance to the world. But as its head pressed against her and she bore down, it was evident that no matter how intent she was on helping her child emerge, the task would not be easy.

Tears and blood streamed as she pushed. Her efforts did not match the child's progress. Worry and fear toiled within her, and she closed her eyes to focus more intently.

A hand pressed against her forehead. Her eyes flashed open. Disappointment sank her eyelids closed. It was the midwife, not the person she'd hoped. The woman must have decided that duty mattered more than a grudge.

"I am a midwife, not a devil," she whispered softly.

Then she guided Raela through the pain.

Raela pushed harder. For some reason, the bloody thumbprint she had pressed upon the prophecy flashed into her mind. If she focused on it and obeyed the midwife's instructions, the task became easier. Time moved slowly, although progress was made.

After one final desperate push, the baby's cries consumed all that was left of her energy. Broken and bloody, she did not move.

At last, the midwife placed the infant in Raela's arms. "A girl," was all she said.

Raela gazed down at her bundle, bright red and distressed. She examined every inch of her baby's scrunched-up face.

A small fist reached for something, and she caught the tiny wrist between her fingers. Though the baby's thumb was small, the birthmark was evident. Raela's child bore the mark that she, herself, possessed upon her thumb. The child had the mark of the scribe—she was now the prophecy's keeper.

Tears sprang from her eyes as she realized the significance of this mark upon her child's thumb. Her grandfather's vision had been clear.

The one bearing the mark must return the prophecy to its rightful place. That the child possessed it meant that she might be the one who did so, not Raela. Which suggested that Rebial may not return. Or that Raela may not be alive to greet him when he did.

The midwife mistook her tears for those of joy, and there may have been some drops that contained it within the murky streams.

"I will leave you two alone," she said before leaving Raela to bear the pain of something more painful than the birth itself.

❧

Rebial had what seemed like several weeks of peace as he alternated between man and forest, vegetation and wood.

Perhaps it was even longer, for time moves like a snail within a forest.

But it was only peaceful in the sense that there were no more intrusions. During these moments the forest concealed his handiwork, allowing leftover bits of men and tools to sink into the ground. Trees encroached—blasting the manmade beasts apart with great limbs. Grasping roots pulled them into crumbling soil. When the forest had consumed most traces of the invaders and their brightly colored objects, a new type of invader came.

They came in greater numbers, wearing clothing that blended more with the forest, although this tactic did not trick Rebial. Perhaps they fooled each other, but he could feel them infiltrating his woods like busy ants, searching for someone or something.

No longer were they tearing down trees or driving soulless beasts in to rip the scenery to shreds. Instead, they moved cautiously between trunks, attempting to be inconspicuous. Hiding in the shrubs and darting around, they seemed to be taking a cue from Rebial's earlier efforts, although only by a fraction. In reality, they were still just clumsy humans invading a space they did not fully understand. Their attempts to evade his knowledge of their whereabouts were unsuccessful.

Unsure as to their intentions, though suspicious, Rebial observed as they flitted back and forth between the trees. When someone found the forgotten shoe of a long-deceased invader, held it up and had a lengthy discussion with nearby men, he knew they were here to avenge the deaths of the men who'd come before them.

Still, these humans did not understand what they were up against. His cats stalked them from behind.

Drawing long bulky cylinders that had been strapped

onto their backs, they aimed these frightful weapons all around before continuing onward.

But Rebial would provide them no easy target. Not yet. He stayed hidden within the eye of the wood. For he was one with the forest now. Even if he materialized, he would not appear as a solid figure. Immersed within a clearing, he waited.

But with his focus so intent on these new invaders, he did not notice the young, female deer that chewed the undergrowth in their vicinity. The fawn traveled within sight of the invaders, watching them from a distance. After careful observation, she finally recognized them as a threat and began to move away. A man caught sight of her galloping figure and aimed his weapon. A loud boom reverberated throughout the wood.

Blood splattered into the air and fell like heavy rain upon the surrounding vegetation. Rebial's temper brewed like a tempest as he felt the blood of one of his own seep into the soil.

The fawn ran in terror as if she could distance herself from her gaping wound. Her fright added to Rebial's fury, poking at him to avenge what would surely be a sudden death. After a short time, the deer's legs would finally stiffen, and she would crash into the undergrowth to die.

The invaders did not even chase their future kill, having shrugged their shoulders once they recognized the fleeing gait of the deer was not one of a man.

This infuriated him, seeing them kill this deer without concern for her spirit. Not only that, but they had killed a female too young to have even borne her own children yet. They had deprived her of her duty to contribute to the cycle of life. This was the deer's last despair-ridden thought as she raced toward death.

His enemies continued to slink through the forest, looking for their next victim. Looking for him. He would not hide. But he also would not make the same mistakes he'd made before.

Strange sounds echoed through the woods as he allowed them to move closer to his spot within the clearing. Small mumblings, tinny voices, projected from tiny boxes. He was certain they were discussing how they would capture him. He'd make it easy on them. They would regret it. His cats waited overhead, having followed through the treetops in anticipation of them finding him.

The enemy moved into the clearing, hundreds of them, each sensing the strangeness of his presence. Their hardened expressions could not hide their bewilderment. Although they could not see him as a man, they saw his entity—bits and pieces of him and the forest intertwined. He made the effort to clarify himself before them, focused on who he had once been, and they finally spotted him.

He knew this because they surrounded where he imagined himself to be. Weapons aimed, they sent streams of pellets toward him. These flying bits ripped into trees, scaring animals farther away. Insects flew away from the resulting smoke. Holes ripped through his flesh which had transformed to vegetation and tree matter long ago. But these pieces of himself only fertilized the soil around him as he endured their attack. His body grew back with vigor.

Their attack swirled his thoughts into a frenzy that united apathy, rage, and passion. Near a cave, an object wrapped in roots pulsed and sent shock waves toward him. Pain ripped through his body. What felt like lightning lit his soul. He screamed—a rasping, blood-curling, electrified cry of war that prevailed over the sound of weapons.

The forest maddened all around them—creaking, groaning, rustling, twisting, becoming gnarled—from the treetops to the farthest reaches of its roots.

Rebial widened, stretched farther than was humanely possible, dispersed into everything. No longer was he here or there, but instead, he was everywhere. He was the wood. He had moved from its eye into its mind. He was now connected to every living thing that belonged there—all at once—controlled them like a flick of his finger, a twitch of his toes.

One last thought riddled through him before he succumbed entirely to his new existence. He would not let them destroy his village, the leftover homes of his tribe and even his own. He would keep it safely tucked away. In Rebial's human mind, he hugged it, but in reality, the surrounding nature overtook it. The entire village became overgrown with leaves and brush, sank beneath roots and trunks of trees. His last bit of humanity sank with it.

Now that he shared the forest's mind, Rebial found he could be in many places at once. For even though a forest is comprised of many things, all the animals and plants, trees and fungus, even the insects, make up the whole. And Rebial was a part of this whole. He was inside every living thing, just the same as they were inside him. This meant that everything inside the forest now shared his mind, his goals, his purpose. They lived to meet his purpose the same way he lived to meet theirs.

Survival. It was all about survival. Evading death for the mere purpose of continuity and upholding each other to benefit the whole.

But now, with Rebial inside it, the forest also was motivated to avenge.

Mercy was no longer something he could fathom. Mercy was not an attribute of a forest.

He would show these invaders no mercy, just the same as their predecessors had ruthlessly felled trees. All of them in their great numbers, matching an army of ants.

Now that he was no longer visible, his enemies knew not where to aim their weapons of destruction. They tore more holes throughout the woods, but their weapons were merely made to still a beating heart, and the heart inside the forest was not one they could touch. They could chop down its trees and kill its animals, but they could not erase its soul.

Through the will of Rebial, great trees moved like fingers, crushing invaders into bits and pieces within muddy palms. Roots roped men's feet to the ground, causing them to topple over and smash their heads against emerging stones. Branches bowed and bent to stab through flesh. Plants grew with speed and vigor to capture an enemy within its tendrils.

As the invaders disbanded to escape what was happening, he changed their whereabouts with a shift in his imagination. For his mind was now the forest and the trees, interchangeable. Which meant that when the forest suffered, Rebial also suffered too. But a forest only suffers for so long. He knew this now. A forest could rejuvenate itself over time. A forest could return.

Tree crowns suctioned downward like spiders, pushing invaders through the dirt to early graves. Canopies bent to sweep invaders from the land. The land trembled and quaked, creating huge gaps within the soil that caused fatal falls.

Cougars appeared with sudden ferocity, biting necks of men who hid. Swarms of insects flew into gaping mouths and ears. These tiny bugs corrupted minds, burrowing into eyes and noses, creating further hysteria.

Mushrooms grew from arms and faces, terrifying victims who ran away screaming. Tree branches dipped down to slice through them. Snakes coiled up legs and torsos to wrap themselves quickly around weapons that no longer provided protection.

Trees mutated into creatures that tore at faces with protruding branches. The strange weaponry the invaders used could open up grisly wounds, but this could only do so much to a tree.

The forest continued changing from different angles. Paths quickly became overgrown with brush and new ones opened. The invaders could not run away when their paths kept disappearing and the scenery became indistinguishable from one vantage point to the next. The river that rushed through the woods ran off course to wash men off their feet and drown them. Returning to its normal path, it carried them into the depths of the wilderness.

Passing thoughts of satisfaction over a kill were like bits of dust covering up piles of human bones.

What transpired was like a living version of a story in his mind. And so it happened—this story—many times, over and over, death and destruction littering his forest, until the invaders finally stopped entering his woods.

CHAPTER THIRTY-TWO

AS A YOUNG mother, Raela continued to pine for Rebial, having faith that at one time he would come.

She rocked her child and daydreamed of a place that was more vibrant than the cold, depressing walls of her cramped space.

According to Rebial, she could always return, but she knew this as only a false hope. The prophecy had bled from her fingers as the seer spoke the wisdom of its words. She had felt the power of these words, the power of his vision. Such things didn't happen if they weren't important.

The story of her grandfather's death had turned into a scandal, as things did when people had nothing to occupy their thoughts. Some claimed Rebial had murdered him out of spite, but she knew her lover's heart was noble even when astray. The damage he was capable of inflicting would not be directed at a weak old man. He would direct it full force toward evil's core and the seer was only the messenger of bad news, not the culprit of it.

Her cheeks burned and her heart thundered in her chest when she heard them speak of him like that. Shouts stormed from her throat. They learned to gossip more discreetly.

She could see him moving through the tunnels. Coming toward her with the purpose and stealth that a warrior as great as he was meant to have. He was covered in moss and blood, a tree branch woven through his clothes. Like always, he was intent on the path before him, pursuing his goal of reaching her.

But she could also sense the prophecy beating steadily like a heart beneath the roots of the tree. It remained where she had left it, which meant he was not coming. Somehow, she knew this imagining was more real, that the prophecy was not inside his traveling pouch, its map being used to find her.

Rebial would not take the time to memorize it. He was a man of the woods—not of words, like her. She knew him as fully as she knew herself. Their bond was strong though it stretched farther and farther between them as time wore on.

And yet, she was also a scribe—the keeper of the prophecy. Her grandfather had been so certain she would succeed at this duty even though so far, she had failed. Would he still look at her with his wise, knowing gaze if he'd been alive to see her leave the book behind? How could she be its keeper when it was no longer in her possession? What did all this mean?

Suddenly, she remembered the last thing she had written on the cave wall, something that may have been more insightful than she realized. What she had written there began to haunt her. She had to check what she'd recorded, see if her memory matched her suspicion.

She also remembered the narrow rift between that spot and the final pathway to their chamber. Once they'd reached their village, the cave had rumbled, and its walls had shaken around them. Some of the men who'd roamed the tunnels after mentioned that their route had changed, was different than before due to the shifting of stone.

She would bring a rope for passage just in case. Not knowing what the extent of their underground journey would entail, the tribe had brought some. The long strands were still coiled in a pile near the entrance to their cavern.

Still, swinging on a rope was not ideal for a child. In fact, it was dangerous. Raela carried her young daughter to the midwife's dwelling. The woman was bent over, mixing herbs in small clay bowls.

She looked up at Raela in her doorway.

"Can you please watch Maali for a short time?" Raela asked.

The midwife stood and dusted her hands. "How short a time?" she asked suspiciously. "For what reason?"

"I need to check something," Raela said, holding her daughter outward.

The midwife seemed hesitant to take the sleeping baby from her mother. "Go and check what? Are you lying to me?"

"No," Raela insisted. "Please. I won't be long. Just take her and keep her safe."

"Why would she not be safe with you?"

"Because I'm going back into the tunnels."

"Back how far?"

Raela suddenly understood the midwife's questioning. "I'm not leaving her forever," she said defensively.

"You left behind the book. Why is it so illogical for me to think that you'd now leave behind your daughter?"

Raela hugged her daughter tightly to her chest. "I would never do that."

"How can I believe you? How can I be sure?"

Raela considered, realizing that she had nothing to offer

the midwife to earn her trust. Instead, she noticed the woven cradle bag resting on the floor next to the woman's supplies.

"You can't," Raela said. "So let me borrow the woven cradle, and I will take her with."

❧

After the midwife helped her wrap little Maali in the woven cradle and strap it to her chest, Raela walked the curved pathways out of the village and stopped at the cavern's entrance. She collected a rope from the pile, wrapped it securely around her waist.

Then she moved back through the cave's tunnels toward the spot where she had etched her last message to Rebial. She had the sneaking suspicion that she would not like what she had written there, but she had to know. She had to verify that her grandfather was correct.

She patted her child's back as she ambled through the tunnels, aware that someone followed, but for some reason unafraid. Years of defiance beneath the ground had strengthened her. No one could harm her more than she had already harmed herself.

Reaching the once narrow gap, its wideness now stretched before her. It was impassable without help, but she had prepared for this. She unwound the rope from around her waist.

Swinging across would remind her of her days with her lover. Together they had played like children in the trees before their interests changed and they partook in other activities on high branches. Little had she known then those times and her loyalty to him would define her to the very end of her life.

There would be no lovers after him, and though she was

lonely, regret never surfaced. Any regret she had was busy dwelling on other things.

As she debated her options, noticing an upturned section of rock on the wall that could serve as a notch, she heard a scuffing sound behind her. Someone now approached, and she whirled to face this invader of her thoughts and space.

It was the man who would not leave her be, no matter how much she ignored him. He still lurked at the outskirts of her consciousness at times, edging slowly past her tiny dwelling, watching with prying eyes as she gathered water or bathed in the shimmering pools outside the village.

But her patience had worn so thin that it had also weakened her resolve to rid herself of him.

"What is it now, Vandor?" she asked.

Frail and weak like the others, his demeanor had become subdued, and perhaps so had his conniving nature. Either way, she did not care. He no longer scared her.

"I can help you across," he said, feigning kindness. "Or perhaps you'd let me hold your child?"

His offer, as always, was loaded with unsaid motivations. He never tired of offering his services, and though she did not trust him, she still decided that his help was better than none.

"Fine," she replied, "I could use your help."

Vandor waddled forward eagerly, gaining a proximity that before she never would have allowed. But his arms still had strength, and she could use that strength, not to hold her daughter, but to help maneuver them across.

He held his arms out to take the child, but she shook her head and reveled in his disappointment.

"You can help us both across," she said. "Take this knot I've made and climb those jagged stones to loop it through the section jutting from the wall."

She pointed and he nodded, resigning to his role.

He climbed awkwardly to where she had directed and looped the knot through the stone that would serve as her hook. Then he returned, looked at her hopefully as she tugged on the end of the rope to ensure it was secure.

He did not ask why she desired to cross the gap, nor did she offer her reasoning. Instead, she asked him to step away and he complied. She wrapped the rope around her wrists, kissed her daughter's head, and swung across to the other side. She landed and fell to her knees from the brunt force of it, but her daughter barely felt the impact so nestled she was against her mother's chest.

Vandor watched from the other side as she stood, shuffling ever closer to the edge and dividing his attention between her and the blackness below.

"I'll be back," she called over the rift, wedging her end of the rope into a crack, "in a few hours. It doesn't matter if you wait."

But she could tell by his hungry expression that he would.

She lit a torch and walked through the dark passages until she found where she'd written the words, scanned them desperately while choking back a breath.

They threaten to kill me for leaving the prophecy. Except only I know the way. I will teach it to our child. She will carry the same burden. So will our descendants until it is done. Only when the prophecy is returned can our spirits sleep. Even though we've altered fate, you should have come. If I don't see you again in this life, I will love you in the next.

She reread them as a strange realization wafted over her, one that contained both recognition and shock.

The words she'd written, thinking she was being poetic and dramatic, had even been an overstretching of the truth, now rang truer than she could believe.

She sank to her knees, wincing from their soreness, and suddenly remembered other things, like deciding to leave the prophecy, although she had never admitted this to herself out loud. And then she'd followed through with doing it, yet still acted as if it were a spontaneous decision. She'd even memorized it beforehand, protecting herself. Known she would carry Rebial's child. Patted her stomach before she'd realized the baby had been conceived.

Even before then, she'd known that the prophecy would be a burden for her children to bear, not herself. Looking down at her daughter, she hoped the burden would not be too great.

And so, she finally acknowledged that her grandfather was correct. She'd had the sight all along but had been too preoccupied to notice.

She staggered back to the rift, the realization of who she was heavy on her conscious. The cold emptiness of the tunnels exacerbated all the thoughts swirling in her head. Her knees throbbed painfully with each step.

Vandor waiting for her on the other side steadied her emotions and sharpened her instincts. Like an excited child, he danced from foot to foot in anticipation. His life truly had been reduced to accepting whatever speck of excitement came his way.

Yet he had come her way once more, and she approached him ever the wiser.

"I waited for you," he said, as if it weren't evident that he'd lingered. "I'm here to help."

She pulled her end of the rope out from the crack, yanked on it to make sure he hadn't somehow loosened it from the wall. Then she prepared herself and said, "Stand back."

"I will catch you," he said, bracing himself along the edge. "That way, you won't land on your knees again."

It was tempting, for her knees now burned from the impact of her previous landing. Glancing down, she noticed that yellow bruises had formed in their most tender spots.

Despite this, she commanded, "Back away from the edge."

Ducking his head like a reprimanded child, he shuffled backward, but only by a few steps.

Sighing, she could see there was no dissuading him. For whatever reason, he wished to help her, although she suspected his form of help would be debatable.

So without warning, she pushed her feet against the stone and swung across.

He rushed to catch them, but instead of attempting to land like a cat upon her feet with his help, she allowed her weight to hit him with full force. They landed heavy like a heap of stone. And yet, her daughter had been attached so snugly to her chest that she stayed protected. Though her tiny eyes did flick open, and she sighed a startled breath.

Vandor's face expressed disappointment as Raela stood and dusted herself off, leaving him sprawled across the ground.

"Thank you, Vandor," she said, moving past him. "But I no longer need your help, so do not offer it again."

One final glance backward caught him gazing forlornly

into the rift, fantasizing, she was sure, about what would have happened had she or Maali ended up there. Or more accurately, had she allowed him to push them ever so gently over the edge.

233

CHAPTER THIRTY-THREE

WHEN IT APPEARED there would be no more intruders in his woods, and he had no enemies to combat, Rebial found that time passed slowly.

To entertain himself, and because a mere thought would inspire it, he intermingled with many creatures. He entered the mind of a squirrel or burrowed as roots at the pace of a snail. He could not even differentiate himself from a snail for that matter.

His mind traveled to forbidden corners that before had been too overgrown to breach. Memories that had transpired in the forest hid there—some satisfying, some unwelcome—but he watched them like moving pictures inside the mind they now shared.

Over the course of many years, many people had created these memories inside his woods—his father, his mother, forgotten ancestors, members of his tribe and those long dead. He even saw the birth of the forest itself when it fell as a seed beneath a giant tree that towered like a god overhead, its canopy seemingly reaching the clouds.

Overwhelmed by this plethora of images, he decided to only focus on his past life.

His thoughts rested on Raela, and he yearned for her stronger than ever before. He saw the experiences they had shared, snippets from their relationship, intimate encounters he'd forgotten about in the trees. They seemed so distant to him now.

The prophecy she had left behind tempted him more each day, but he could not bring himself to concede to its attraction. Although he knew it might still be possible to rejoin the tribe, for the mind of a forest is no stranger to new beginnings, he could not bring himself to betray his pride. If anything, she should come back to him.

Instead of sharing the village that now nestled deep within a pocket of the woods, they could both become one with the forest.

Ironically, he now knew how it felt to have the mind of an insect. He had experienced the mindset of a stone. His joining with the woods had clarified such things to him. And yet, he'd mocked these things as insignificant before the tribe's departure. Now he knew these sensations were nothing to scoff at, for insects had camaraderie. A stone had potential in its future. And he had neither.

He did not know how much time had passed since she had gone. He did not know how much more time he could withstand being alone.

His cougars still roamed the woods like passing thoughts, but they no longer interacted with him. Perhaps they could not see him.

Deep in some neglected burrow that now housed his desires, he knew his bond with the forest had grown too strong. Whether this truth was physical or existed only within the mind they shared was hard to determine without trying to break free. Though he suspected testing that theory might kill him, for now, when he scratched his head, a tree branch brushed against a cliff. When he stood tall, he actually did reach the sky.

Him leaving the woods would be like a soul exiting its body—impossible except in death.

The prophecy remained beneath the tree as a twisted idea, a memory he could not erase nor ever fully wipe clean. Somehow, he knew it had something to do with his merging with the wood, but how and why he could not fathom. It should have no fondness for him since he'd disobeyed its wishes. He continued to have no fondness for it except for the mere fact that Raela had left it behind for him.

Although the forest was now peaceful and untouched, he only experienced pure satisfaction when he slept. He dreamt mainly about his life before the prophecy had been created when Raela was destined to be his wife and the tribe inhabited the wood. He dreamt about the big cats' solid statures accompanying him on his daily walks. He dreamt about himself when he was only a man and not an extension of the wood—or at present, the wood itself.

So to pass the time and ease his mind, Rebial fell into a deeply obscure slumber in which the happenings in the forest were like subtle whims and fancies in a dream.

And as Rebial, the forest slept too.

Which was why he did not sense the intrusion. Something flew overhead, bigger than a bird and with wings that did not flap, dropping several objects onto his head—the canopy of the woods. Each resembled the rigid body of a fish. They swam partway through the maze of twigs and leaves before exploding—Deafening bangs that ruptured the planet.

His forest blew apart in all directions. Rebial's insides

imploded as trees shattered into bits. Rocks and bark blasted across many miles. Large craters marred his soil like imperfections of the skin. Fire rose as grisly monsters and spread ferociously, consuming vegetation.

And the forest cringed in pain. Over and over again until he felt himself compress into a separate being. It was unbearable, feeling himself crop up so painfully again as only a blend of forest and man. His lungs now the opposite of what they were, he coughed within the smoke. Lifted a hand that he could barely see. And decided he better move.

Ignoring the scent of vaporized animals and singed plant life, he began to run. As fire raged at his heels, he remembered his previous skill. He scanned his blurry mind and found a spot unaffected by the assault. Imagining himself in that safer place, he went there.

But this area was shaded and gloomy, as if it knew what had happened many miles away. Sitting on a stump, inside only his body once again, grief over the ruin he'd just escaped from overtook him. He mourned the loss of his trees, the animals, the vegetation, but most of all he mourned his union with the wood.

And he knew then that the mind of the forest was similar to his own mind now that he'd been inside it. He sensed its pain as if it were his own. Had he not been driven out he could have seen it all.

Yet this invasion had been unforeseen. No men accompanied it. This worried him. And now his mind felt vacated and riddled with too much space, allowing this worry to grow.

He thought he'd succeeded in keeping his woods safe, but this new form of invasion proved that he'd missed something. And perhaps his staying behind had not made things better for his homeland, but instead had hurried something along, something that he did not have the capacity to fix.

The prophecy badgered his senses, its presence in the wood unforgotten. The impact it had upon his forest was a conundrum, for it had foretold of its destruction. When before he had saved his homeland, today it suffered. Yet within that suffering, the prophecy remained and so did he. And no matter how hard he tried, he could not drive the book from his mind.

CHAPTER THIRTY-FOUR

RAELA FOUND THAT her daughter brightened the small bleak room they called their own within the village. A few of Maali's trinkets lined the walls—a doll made from bits of cloth with a face as blunt as stone, a green herb with tiny flowers that the midwife had given her, a pile of rocks stacked in the shape of a hut.

Holding Maali in her lap, she patted her child's wispy black hair. Maali gazed up at her mother adoringly, round-faced and innocent. Her large, brown eyes did not share the pain that Raela was sure her own emitted at times. She was glad she had not infected her young daughter with her own despair. It was the one satisfaction she clung to in life.

"Do you remember?" she asked the child.

"Yes, Mother," Maali said. "I remember what you've told me."

"Very good," she replied. "I am so proud of you. Now please repeat your task aloud. Tell me the way."

"I will not," Maali said in her tiny voice, "ever say my secret out loud. I will never tell anyone the way out of the cave."

"Very good again. And why not?"

"Because of this." The girl held up her thumb and grinned.

Raela smiled back. She had emphasized to her daughter the mark's importance. She was happy Maali had listened.

"And if anyone begs it from you or threatens?"

"I will be as strong as you and Father," Maali said. "I will not reveal my secret."

"Except to who?" Raela asked.

"Except to my own daughter, when I am old like you."

Raela smiled again, not feeling old in her twenty-two years. "Who else might you tell?"

"I will tell the people," she replied, "but only when it's time and under one condition."

"And what would that condition be?"

"If a vision tells me to do so. Only then will I lead them free."

Raela hugged her daughter close, so proud of Maali she was. But she also felt the sorrow of leaving such a task to her very young daughter.

"I regret that you will carry this burden, but it must be. And if you do your job, I believe the world will be a better place for it. Not to mention you'll secure the future of our tribe."

"I know, Mother," Maali said softly. "And I will."

"Now again, recite what I have taught you. But do it in your secret voice."

And so again, the child whispered the words into her mother's ear.

⁌

The darkness Raela and the tribe experienced when they slept was absolute inside a cave, without the moon to soften any edges. It even enhanced their nightmares.

"Mother," screamed Maali, jolting Raela awake beside her.

The child was several years older now and not yet prone to waking in the night.

"What's wrong," Raela hissed, shaking Maali's shoulders, hoping to wake her more completely before she disturbed the others.

Maali's eyes blinked open slowly. "I had a dream, Mother."

"Tell me in your secret voice," Raela said as she stroked her daughter's forehead.

"I don't understand it," Maali whispered.

"What was it about?"

"It was about a place," Maali replied.

This startled Raela, for her daughter had not seen any places outside the cavern that housed their village. She hadn't even been taken back into the tunnels.

"What place? Can you describe it?"

"I don't know how," Maali's voice trembled, "but somehow, perhaps because it was a dream, I knew that it was above ground."

Raela cringed at the thought of her daughter dreaming about places that she hadn't even been alive to see and may never be alive to see. It also made the blackness surrounding them all the more foreboding.

"What did the place look like?"

"It was beautiful," Maali replied. "At least, it was at first."

Raela's heart thudded in her chest.

"There were many tall pillars—taller than the formations that drip inside our cave—but with brown bodies and knobby, straggly legs. They had many arms and green chunks of hair." Her daughter's voice grew more urgent. "These pillars were alive, I know this, even though they had no faces. They were being killed one by one, cut straight through their bodies. But instead of bleeding from their wounds, they just toppled over."

Raela grabbed her daughter's hand, willing her to continue.

"I think it's what you called a forest," Maali said, "the place where you were born. And it was dying."

"Our homeland," Raela said. "Your true homeland."

"I can't get their screams out of my head."

Raela was surprised by this. "They were screaming?"

"Yes," she replied as if this were not unusual, "and when they fell, they shook the planet."

Raela wondered when she'd taught her daughter such a word, but something else piqued her curiosity even more. "Was there…did you also see a person?" she asked tentatively.

"I did, but he was not like you and me."

"What do you mean?" Raela asked fearfully.

Tortured images of Rebial sprang into her mind.

"He was part forest and part man. Is there such a creature, Mother?"

Raela took the information in, not knowing how to respond. Was her daughter's imagining just a dream or was it real? It was difficult to determine what could be a vision and what was not. And there was no one but herself to consult with. She was the granddaughter of the seer. But she was also the scourge of the tribe. And even if someone were familiar with the legitimacy of visions inside dreams, they would surely not discuss anything with her.

"There wasn't when I lived there," Raela said. "But perhaps there is now. What does he look like?"

"He looks angry," Maali said. "I do not know if he is kind. But he protects the trees."

This statement caused Raela much pain, and she squeezed her daughter's shoulder. "He would protect you too."

"How do you know?" Maali asked. "He does not like the other men inside the forest."

"What are the men doing? What do they look like?"

"They look different than the men of the tribe. And they are attacking the trees."

"Then that's why the forest man is angry," Raela said. "A forest is too beautiful to destroy. And I know he would protect you because he is your father."

"That was my father?" Maali asked in disbelief. She raised a hand and stared at her fingers. "Is the forest also part of me?"

"No," Raela responded, pulling her daughter close, "you are all little girl."

"Why did he stay behind?" Maali asked, squirming away.

"He is protecting our homeland," Raela said, pride tinging her voice.

Maali was silent for a moment, seemingly bothered by something. "But that was a long time ago."

"What do you mean?" Raela asked, confused by the certainty in her daughter's voice.

"The forest looks different now," she said grimly.

Raela shivered. Surely Rebial was still alive…

"How do you know?" she asked.

"Because you know things like that in dreams," Maali replied, as if she were an expert.

"Well then," Raela said cautiously, "what does it look like now?"

Perhaps if her daughter described the place more fully, she would find her father.

"It looks empty."

"Empty?" Raela tried to imagine her flourishing forest as empty, but her mind fell short. "Where is your father?"

Perhaps this was a sign that he was on his way. Her heart lifted as she considered this in the brief moment before Maali spoke again.

"He's still there," she replied.

Her hopes dashed just as quickly as they'd risen, she asked, "What is he doing?"

"I don't know. I do not see him."

Raela tried to keep her voice from shaking. "How do you know he's still there if you can't see him?"

"Because you just know things like that in dreams," Maali said again, burying her face into her pillow.

Raela stroked Maali's head and stayed up the rest of the night ruminating over her daughter's frightful vision.

৵

Maali's dreams grew more intense as she aged, worsening into nightmares. The child that Raela had prepared to lead the others became consumed by her task. She woke screaming in the night, stirring the others, causing those who had grown heartless to insist that the child should have been disposed of as the elders had suggested—that she was more of a burden than a help.

They moved farther away from the center of the village where Maali and her mother lived. Some even went so far to say that wherever the child went, they would rather not follow.

Devastated by guilt, Raela paced beside Maali as she slept, unable to rest with her, waiting for the moment when she'd awaken and cry out. That way, she could calm her before she woke the rest of the tribe.

At least Maali seemed happy during waking hours. Her face had thinned in a pleasant sort of way, her hair now silky and long. She was more than just a child suffering from nightmares, no matter what the others said. Maali liked to help the midwife and gathered water for the others. She even told her stories about the forest to the other children, although some were not allowed to play with her.

But one night, Maali wakened, panting wildly and whimpering soft tears.

"What is it?" Raela asked, already kneeling beside her.

She placed her hand on her daughter's cool forehead.

"You were in my dreams, Mother," Maali said, tears streaming down her face. "You were showing me to the forest I can't get to."

An uneasiness came over Raela, even though dreams are known to be independent. One cannot influence the dreams of another. At least not without meaning to. And she would never impact her daughter's dreams like that.

"I'm sorry," she said softly, "but it was just a dream."

"You showed me something beneath a tree," Maali continued. "For some reason, I was afraid."

Raela choked back a breath and coughed.

"Mother, what is beneath the tree?"

Guilt crawled in, replacing her worry. "It's a book," she whispered. "The book your father may still bring us."

"But he won't, Mother. I know he won't."

"How do you know?"

"Because after you placed it there, you merely paced within the darkness. You wouldn't stop. You paced over and over in my mind until I got dizzy."

Raela recoiled, disturbed by this revelation. Apparently, Maali sensed what she was doing every night before she collapsed in fatigue.

"I think you would have done so forever if I hadn't woken up." Maali began to cry again. "It was terrible."

"I realize," Raela said, "that your dream was unpleasant, but I'm not sure why it's making you cry."

"It went on and on. I thought it would never end. I couldn't make you stop no matter how I tried. And I've come to realize that my pain and suffering, these torments I endure inside my head…"

Raela felt lightheaded, fearing what came next.

"They're because of you."

Her daughter's eyes shot accusations at her. Raela could not tell her daughter that she was wrong.

"I am your tool, Mother," Maali continued bitterly. "And I will carry this burden forever."

Her daughter's words cut sharper than Rebial's sharpest knife. They expressed what she had always known was true, and she'd allowed it to happen. She had cursed her daughter to relieve herself of the burden she had been chained to. So resistant to be a tool herself, she'd passed that burden on to the one person that was most precious to her besides Rebial.

Yet her daughter was the living, breathing person right beside her. Maali, so helpless yet strong-willed like both her father and her mother, would suffer greatly for their mistakes.

❧

Unlike Rebial, who did not join the tribe, Maali's dreams continued to come again and again. The irony was not lost on Raela, who worried less and less over Rebial, so she could focus her worries more so on her daughter.

"I must return it, Mother. I must return it to its rightful place." Maali lay beside her mother in the blackness, the desperation in her voice breaking Raela's heart.

The girl was not quite yet a teenager but was nearing the age of greater independence. Except Raela knew that she was trapped within the confines of her burden. She could feel the bitterness brewing inside her daughter, knew that her resentment would only worsen.

"You must, but now is not the time," she said in a voice attempting to console.

"But if I can't return it, then these dreams will never stop."

Raela consulted the midwife then, hoping that her only friend possessed an herb that could cure her daughter of her troubles.

It was one thing to be destined to carry out a task, quite another to be tormented by the burden.

The midwife did offer an herb to help Maali sleep throughout the night. Though she still tossed and turned, she did so with less vigor. Her eyes stayed tightly shut.

And so Raela thought the herb had worked and found a semblance of peace living with Maali, who no longer cried out during the night. Her pleasant demeanor during the day transformed into one that was solemn and reflective. She looked older, wiser, and less focused on childish ways to enjoy herself.

She assumed it was her daughter's age that changed her, as logic formed to help organize her thoughts. But after several days, she realized she was wrong.

"Stop bothering me inside my head," Maali said to her one morning in a bossy voice as they made jewelry together.

Raela paused, awl in one hand, bead in the other. "Whatever do you mean?"

"You pace around and never stop. It hurts. It bothers me. I do not like it."

Raela felt the same way about her daughter's accusing tone. "Well, I am sorry that's the case, but there's not much I can do to stop it."

"If you hadn't cursed me," Maali said with a scowl, "then I could dream like other people and not have this heavy weight upon my chest."

"You still have those dreams?" she asked, the guilt she experienced every day now rolling inside her.

"Of course, I do," Maali said, impatience brimming her words. "It's just now I can no longer wake up. I'm forced to endure them every night, and they always end with you pacing about inside my head."

Raela stopped giving her daughter the herb. Maali woke up again throughout the night and stopped looking to her mother for comfort.

And Raela now mourned her daughter's predicament instead of Rebial's absence, for Maali's personality was now tainted by what she called a curse. And Raela wondered if this was true since her daughter was so insightful, for she remembered the blood ritual she and Rebial had undergone.

Perhaps it had perpetuated something unforeseen that had made matters even worse. And she hated herself for mingling her blood with that of her lover's and pressing it onto the book.

So she watched her daughter grow into a woman who did not daydream with the same carefree wonder that she'd possessed as a child. And knew it was all her fault.

CHAPTER THIRTY-FIVE

THERE WAS A span of calmness marred by all the past death as Rebial's forest struggled to heal itself from the last invasion. And when it almost did, a different threat surfaced. It came from the sky. It came from all around them. And this time, nothing flew overhead to bring it. The arrival was invisible.

This was a new threat, one Rebial did not have the prowess to counter.

Poisons. Polluted air. The planet's sickness encroached upon his forest. His trees could no longer breathe. The sun's rays were too harsh. Air no longer nourished. Heat suffocated everything like a burning cloak. As a result, distant forests met death by wildfire.

Vegetation became straggly and sparse, bitten down into skeletons by starving insects. The once lush undergrowth now died fast. Before long, it was gone completely. The dirt where it had grown was now crumbly like sand.

Plants wilted and did not grow back. His forest wizened, shriveled up, as did he. Rebial felt his own lungs struggling. They no longer felt relief with normal breath but pain during each inhale and exhale. He felt the disease and sickness, but in a way much different than he had ever experienced such things before.

The woods growing weaker brought the emergence of insects that liked to burrow and invade in ways that were more deadly than the men who caused their arrival.

This was also when the remainder of the animals died out or left. He found a big cat stiff and rotting one day. The others either spent their last moments hiding underground or had parted ways with his homeland. Perhaps one had even burned in the fire. Their deaths caused him to grow lonelier than he ever conceived possible. He missed them stalking him throughout the day, swift on his heels with their tails coiled around him when he paused, their strong animal scent bathing his senses. He missed their warmth at night.

Even the spirits of his ancestors drifted away, the ones who hadn't disappeared completely when destruction ruled the wood. Forced to roam the land like ghosts, these faded remnants were now tainted, as everything above ground was tainted.

When the trees started dying, he became overwhelmed. Their leaves fell and decayed. Trunks crumbled before his eyes and laid in ashen heaps on the forest floor. Others remained as jagged planks of bark, reminding him of hollowed bones jutting from the dirt.

At this point, he was barely hanging on himself. His breath had long escaped him, and soon his spirit withered like the trees.

When he was ready to return to his thoughts where she existed, when he really needed her to be there, when the poisons were tormenting him though he would not die, her memory was gone.

Recovery looked bleaker than the saddest remains of a tree. And finally, he understood.

He had fought the battle and had stood just as powerfully as the trees—or rather, he had been the trees—but he'd still ended up tainted. Like he'd been beaten at something when he wasn't paying attention. As if there had been an object to the game he had not been aware of until now. Perhaps he had won the war but had still lost something in return.

He was too proud to cater to the thought. He just remained, and that was all.

Feeling himself grow ugly, he hated what little piece of existence he had left. He dragged his tired, ragged body into the remnants of a trunk. It took his shape, guarding his spirit in its roots. Then the forest withered and dried up until all that was left was a thick mat of roots beneath the ground.

Memories of the forest and Rebial remained since they were one and the same, within these roots embedded in the soil. The prophecy remained entangled within the roots, like a weak heartbeat that refused to die, hanging on, keeping the underground structure alive and waiting.

Its emblem shone within the dust and dirt, coiling as a never-ending spiral with its beginning and end obscured.

CHAPTER THIRTY-SIX

THE MIDWIFE WENT to the elder one day, disturbed by what she considered dangerous for everyone. Her compassion hurt so much it bled over the plight of the two females whom she was both close to and estranged from. As they all were in many ways.

She had continued watching over Raela and her daughter, as she did for all the women she had cared for with her skills. Seeing how much the pair suffered, she thought it was time for the tribe to show forgiveness.

"She won't stop pacing," the midwife told the elder.

"She must regret her choice."

"She may, but that's no upbringing for her daughter."

"Neither is a life without a father."

"Maali is pleasant by day but distressed every night. She wakes from nightmares routinely. And this fear is creeping into her during waking hours. She fears she will go the same route as her mother."

"Can you coax from her the way out of the cave? Can you compel her to write it down? Tell her that it's for the best in case she does go that same route?"

"So you would have me make it worse for her then," the

midwife said. "That knowledge is the only thing they have. It protects them."

"We can't protect one for the cost of many. Perhaps you should persuade Maali to tell you."

"I've tried," the midwife mumbled, "but she refuses to disclose what she has been trained to conceal."

"Too bad," the elder said, "or we could rid ourselves of both."

"I did not tell you this because I want you to commit a crime. But surely the people will have pity on the pair and forgive them."

"It will take many generations before Raela's crime is forgotten. Perhaps once we've journeyed back above ground, once people see the sun again, the treacheries of our past can stay buried beneath our feet."

"I fear we'll all be long dead by then," the midwife said.

But the elder did not argue, for he also knew this as truth.

✍

When her mother died young, Maali thought her grief would be softened by a newfound peace. But Raela's death only killed her physical body. Somehow her spirit remained alive, most often manifesting inside Maali's mind. Every dream she endured was accompanied by her mother pacing endlessly—a pacing in some form of existence kept alive by the prophecy that remained intact within the thick mat of roots beneath the soil. Though the book was many miles away, it sustained Raela's memory and would continue to do so until someone returned it to its rightful place.

Maali knew this, for she had argued with the book on many occasions. It did not talk back, though its symbol gleamed and coiled. Oh, how she'd tried, inside these dreams, to pull the book free. But the roots were wound too strongly around it. If she snapped one, another always grew back in its place. Over and over, she'd try until the task became so tedious that she'd go back to watching her mother pace.

Sometimes she'd search for her father in this strange thing called a forest. Perhaps she could cajole him to bring them the book after all. But he was unapproachable in her dreams, though his mysterious presence remained. This man she'd never met who proved so interesting only existed in some altered state she could not fully grasp. Over time, she gave up.

Every morning she would awaken feeling restless and troubled, her only solace was knowing the truth of why her dreams tormented her. How alarming it would be if her mother had not been alive to explain the reason.

In her waking hours, she had long accepted her fate as the keeper of a book she could not retrieve. She knew she must repeat to her own daughter what her mother had ingrained into her mind. Yet she feared no man would want this burden of a wife.

She spent her days helping the new midwife to give herself something to do that would occupy her thoughts. But she was not meant to treat and cure. The herbs did not obey her. And to most, she was not a peaceful presence.

Except one day, there was a man who did find joy in her presence.

"He only likes me out of duty," she had confided to the midwife. "The tribe has asked him to be my husband."

This hurt her to say aloud, for she was attracted to his clever face and charming ways.

"I do not think so," the midwife had responded. "He would not stumble over his words the way he does around you if he did not have feelings."

Maali watched the midwife soak two herbs together— one with slender green stalks, the other with large oval leaves.

"I am a woman who is not allowed to marry," the midwife said, not looking up. "You should go to him and not find reasons to overthink your lot in life."

And so she did, the midwife nudging her along when doubt crept in.

And eventually, she started her own family with this man who brought her pleasure in life. Forced to continue the curse, Maali never forgave her mother for the nightmares that would plague her own daughter.

She did, however, try to prepare her daughter by showing her what a forest might look like using plants and stone. She wrapped stems around a tiny, flattened rock so the imagery that would appear in her daughter's dreams wouldn't seem so foreign and strange.

They'd sit together on the floor, and Maali would enact a scene with these props along with her daughter's stone-faced doll.

"And so someday in the future, after we lead our people from the cave," Maali told her, "one of us will find the prophecy and bring it here as nature intended."

Her sweet daughter played along with wide and curious eyes. "We will do this, Mother."

As a small child, Maali's daughter was delighted by the story, even wrapped her own flat stone in plant stems that she placed beneath her pillow. When she began to have the dreams, Maali did the best she could to help her daughter cope. And she felt pride knowing that she had lightened the burden.

Every daughter that came after continued to be plagued by this memory of Raela leaving the prophecy inside a forest or pacing inside a cave. It was almost as if to remind them, a way to ensure that what the prophecy had required would come to pass.

Once Raela's family tree grew, only certain daughters were born with the mark. Yet there was always one chosen, whose internal sight was more refined than the others, who would begin to have the visions informing her of the duty.

But this duty became reduced over time. Dreams came and went to varying degrees of urgency. Soon the future was only about returning above ground—the prophecy inside a forest forgotten.

But nature did not forget. And it did not relieve them of their duty.

CHAPTER THIRTY-SEVEN

WHEN THOUGHTS COULD form, they came racing forth, aligned with the girl who suddenly found herself moving quickly toward an opening, rising within molten rock. A womb of magma churned beneath her, pushing her through the bubbling caldera—as if she were being born.

Luma burst through the mouth, streaks of fire shooting into the sky and zigzagging all around her. Then she floated gently down the slope.

More lava gushed forth, raining down on her as she lolled within it, feeling smug, for reasons she could not pinpoint.

The emotion itself was not one she was familiar with, having been so recently born, but somehow, she knew this was the one that most defined her. And with lava continuing to swirl and cascade around her, she sensed she had ridden on the tail end of its triumph.

Something simmered in the background of her thoughts—something she had taken part in when she was more fire than girl. Even if this something happened before she was conscious, it was still an action that she shared with the perpetrator. And because of this, she and fire would remain each other's greatest friend.

It had ravaged the land before her. She knew this just as surely as she could count her fingers and toes. She'd had a role in it, but with things obscured before this moment, the true extent at this point was uncertain. This did not, however, stop her from assuming that her contribution had been great.

And suddenly, she understood what smugness was since it defined her reaction to what she was experiencing.

The volcano brewing nearby was much like her smugness, an emotion she was compelled to bear forever. She knew inside her heart what she had done, felt satisfaction from it. It did not matter whether she had been aware, for pride from her involvement coursed through her veins just as the lava flowed in rivulets away from where she sat. It enlivened her, gave her life and energy.

But she was not done. There were finishing touches she must attend to, for even fire by itself is not always so thorough. It must contend with air and water, crumbling cliffs of stone. Flames could leap and bound across rivers, but it did not always feel inclined to do so. Sometimes motivations such as these went up in smoke.

So it was time for her to traverse the planet to scorch and destroy what no longer served a purpose. She blazed across the land, burned up all the crooked and sick vegetation, wooden dwellings that marred the landscape with their ugliness, great swathes of insects that now ranged out of control. She also burned other things that only added to the sickness in the air, inherently aware that sometimes things must get worse before they can improve.

She burned this and that while she grew taller and

thicker, into what a lash of fire whispered into her ear was called a woman. Her features brought beauty to the smug look, made it more refined.

Then she slipped into a rubbery, swirling dress that had formed from viscous fluid beside her home volcano. Sitting on the edge of her caldera, legs swung over the side, she watched her brothers and sister inspire a lush and verdant greenness to return across the land, growing back in the freshly blackened spots that she had created for this very purpose.

❧

The young boy had ridden the wind longer than he could remember. Wings flapping triggered this thought inside Atmos's mind. Atop the bird, he willed it to dip and dive as he slowly took in the nature of the breeze. It ebbed and flowed and surged. It also traveled like a hasty puff of breath.

The bird dove at an angle that caused him to tumble off, but he soon righted himself in the air, becoming one with the breeze. At first, he merely rode the wind, a passenger as he'd been with the bird. No longer with a bird, but as a wispy boy.

He rolled and glided with an ease that far exceeded the bird, for it had only suggested who he was, taught him who he would become. His knowledge of this flew strong and true. And like any good pupil, he surpassed his teacher with ease.

He gusted here and there across the planet. Though this partnership was not as smooth a wind as one might think, for it was jagged and unpredictable at times, in ways that were quite sudden. Thereafter, the boy discovered that his bond with the wind was stronger as a *going with the flow* type of endeavor, instead of one that could be strictly controlled.

For taking charge of something already on its way was more effective than changing it entirely. It was easier to embrace the wind and guide it along than it was for him to change it.

This is when he truly soared, when he let go and merely suggested to the wind which direction it should turn. Most of the time, it listened, but when it didn't, he enjoyed these bursts of spontaneity.

There were times the wind aided in directing his sister's fire, making it more effective in its journey to rid the planet of tainted things.

Atmos danced with the breeze to diffuse the poisons that his sister's fire ejected into the air. He gathered the toxins floating about with his own breath. He inhaled the giant cloud of pollution swarming the planet and expelled it back into space devoid of poisons and chemicals. He even blew at the oceans for fun and watched his breath skip across the waves.

The planet took a giant breath and then sighed with relief, for now life could begin again. The destruction that had overwhelmed its lands now seemed overblown.

His brother pushed the trees and plants again from the soil. Able to breathe again, they grew lush with vegetation rich with nutrients. They expelled oxygen that would provide clean air to breathe for the creatures that would soon repopulate the planet.

And when he was finally done, the work he'd so joyfully partaken in had left him weathered. So as an old man, Atmos smiled at his adventures and waited for his brother and sisters to finish theirs, so they could tell their stories and watch the world flourish around them.

❧

A bulge emerged from barren soil. Dusty pebbles opened into eyes. The bulge grew into a rounded lump that became larger, taller, finally taking the shape of a young boy. Baric's consciousness took form when his entire body became exposed to light.

He dislodged himself by cracking the soil and dusted the bugs from his skin. He ripped a plant from his arm, but before tossing it, placed one of its berries into his mouth and reveled at the freshness on his tongue. Yes, he was here to renew that sensation in everything around him.

He wobbled to a standing position, stood unsteady for a moment, and began padding lightly across the dry, yellow ground. Itchy grass, haggard from the tribulations it had endured, scratched his feet in greeting. Gnarled branches bent to pat his head. Plants perked up and turned shades of green. Flowers bloomed and opened up as he passed.

Insects welcomed him in strange, whirring voices. Creatures peeked from dens and holes as he traveled through the sprouting forest. Some came forth to say hello while others followed at a distance.

The sun bathed everything in light, informing him of the reason for his existence. It was the driving force of creation after all.

The forest he was born to was similar to one inside a faded dream that he could not fully visualize. This was his home, yet he knew it was not the only forest in existence. He may even have an attachment to another quite like it, but this past life or remembrance could not be fully grasped.

He felt the connection and knew that his understanding would grow, for time clarified things. His surroundings would fill the gaps inside his head eventually with what had transpired before his emergence. This ability to trust the nature of things was ingrained within him.

Massive fire-ravaged buildings marred the skyline as they crumbled beneath it. Baric inspired bands of mushrooms to grow there and engulf them, to break them down and further hurry their demise. Plants encroached to hide these remains from view.

Baric formed animals from clay and sent them running into the wilderness, beckoned others from burrows and forgotten tunnels.

He added fertility to the soil with mycelium that branched from the bottoms of his feet, nudged roots to disperse it throughout the layers. Bugs formed tunnels that would further enhance this endeavor.

After many miles, he reached an area where a thick mat of roots lay hidden underground, waiting to be reinvigorated. These roots seemed to contain their own powerful energy, yet he decided not to inspire them to grow. His decision was inherent, for some reason, he just knew it would be best.

For nature's motives were buried in some remote pocket in his mind, and this knowledge he accepted without question. It was not time for the trees of this forest to reemerge. So he retreated before he could tempt fate and trigger their rebirth.

And so he populated the rest of the planet with greenery and life with the aid of his brother and his sisters. After he had encouraged all that had once lived and died upon the planet to nourish the soil and start the cycle of life again, he found he'd grown into a man. And then he watched what was already inherent in his mind mature and grow just as vast and endless as his surroundings.

❧

The young girl found herself suspended, floating gracefully inside an ocean streaked with light. She spun with playful strokes, making waves, before she propelled herself to swim. As she navigated the water, it turned from brown to clear until settling on a deep blue that merely reflected the sky above them.

Oc~ea joined a school of fish whose movements became more in harmony with one another as she paddled with them. But she had arms and not fins, so she didn't stay for long. She veered into an underground tunnel lined with plants that became more robust as she passed through.

She called creatures from the depths, swimming alongside whales and dolphins, adhering to their swift change of direction as if she were one of them. She also circled with the sharks, though only briefly, for she preferred to float majestically instead.

As she rounded a wide curve, a peculiar-looking glob of something stretched before her. Thick appendages protruded eerily like dead fingers, alongside polyps looming gray and desolate. A ripple of acknowledgment told her this graveyard was a mass of exoskeletons. Deader than death itself, she also knew this large body of mass did not belong as it appeared.

And so she touched it, causing colors to spread across in bright patches until it thrived with life and vigor. What was once stiff and unmoving reanimated and swayed. The coral reef revived made her smile with delight.

Fish wriggled forth from all directions and immersed themselves within the corals. Underwater creatures swam from tunnels to rejoin this underwater forest. Plants grew, providing suitable places for smaller life to flourish. Even places that looked empty now had inhabitants once she peered more closely.

Above her, a giant fish jumped from the water now that the air was safe and splashed back in, joyous that the planet's health had returned.

Oc-ea dove and swam into channels and deep underwater pools so she could reawaken all the creatures and rejuvenate every reef and plant.

As she drifted along, a suspicion swelled inside her thoughts, causing her to pause and slowly sink. Treading to stay afloat, she supposed she might not be the only one just like herself beneath the waters. For she felt a presence deep within an underwater cave that watched her from afar. But with her surroundings so clear around her now, she knew this presence did not need her help. So she decided to keep swimming.

Coming upon a box of half-buried treasure poking from the sand, Oc-ea pulled an aqua-colored gown out from within. She held it up and was surprised to find that it would fit, for she was taller than she'd been when she'd begun. So she pulled it on over her head and admired its flow around her.

Then she swam to a large rock where she could perch and watch her sister and brothers finish revitalizing the planet. She planned to only leave her realm from time to time. Not that it wasn't beautiful up top, but her ocean was even more vast with hidden secrets, ancient ruins, and creatures that only her eyes would see for many years to come.

MANY YEARS LATER, when the small girl plagued by dreams led them above ground, the tribal members had no remembrance of the life they had once lived there. The girl did not remember even why her dreams served as their map. Or why her dreams had finally prompted her to lead her people away from the underground cavern they had resigned themselves to for so long. They had lived inside the planet for so many decades in total darkness that the concept of an alternate origin had vanished.

Perhaps there had been no beginning, and if there was a way to describe it with words, then it was the planet's depths that was their source of origin. Even their perception of time had vanished. Many generations had come and gone. Long ago, stories from the past had stopped being retold, and their remnants faded from every memory over time.

So many years had been spent looking to the future that the past was locked inside itself, no longer accessible.

The child pointed to the jagged opening that she'd seen inside her vision. They crawled out one by one. When the light struck them, they were momentarily blinded and retreated just far enough for comfort. They lived on the cusp for some time until their eyes adjusted. When this occurred, the world they saw was new to them—a magnificent prize. They cherished the beauty around them and knew it deserved their reverence.

Although they never forgot the dirt underneath their feet was sacred, that the girl had shown them the way, they did eventually forget the traveling they had undergone to reach their present situation. New stories of origin were created. They were not supposed to be taken literally. They knew they had come from the planet but forgot the reason why they had lived inside it for so long. This truth had been left behind.

As they had believed for so many years, with their culture suspended in time, they were a people meant to advance. They had waited underground for too long. Now that they lived again beneath the sun, they did not look back. Progress now ingrained within them, they prospered and flourished.

But there was always a troubled child whose dreams portrayed a fading memory that could not be relieved. She would pester her mother and father, beg them for a chance to venture inside a forest so she could find some long-forgotten secret, but they would only quiet her ambitions. And eventually, they were frowned upon, for one should not give too much credence to dreams when there were better things to pursue—things that would enhance their civilization and benefit the tribe.

There was much to learn in this new world they created. And there was no reason to align one's motivations with curiosities and dreams and visions that could not be proved, for there was no such thing as hidden secrets inside the woods.

Though eventually, the child's time would come.

Thank you for reading Wizen Woods. If you enjoyed this book, please consider leaving an honest review. I appreciate the time you take to do this!

You can also receive a *free short story* based on characters in the Immortal Roots series by signing up for my newsletter at www.velvetdavis.com

ALSO BY VELVET DAVIS

Immortal Roots
Dream Relic

Short story series
Space Frivolity
Cataschism
Lunar Logic

ACKNOWLEDGMENTS

Writing a book is a journey that entails many twists and turns. I'd like to thank all the people who helped me out along the way. Thank you to my husband for giving me ideas on how to make Rebial's character even more special. Thank you to Jolivia Porter and Stephanie Vallez for your meaningful support. Each of you contribute your own unique and helpful perspective. I appreciate you both so much and feel lucky to have you as my friends. I'd also like to thank my beta readers for their useful insights, and my editor for such meticulous work. Lastly, I'd like to thank my cover design company for the amazing job they do in designing covers that truly match the essence of my books.